CRIME FICTION

CRIME FICTION

UEA MA
Creative Writing Anthologies
2022

CONTENTS

Foreword

I believe that crime fiction just overtook romance as the most popular genre with UK readers. Or maybe the two categories are still locked in a back-and-forth struggle for the top spot. I'm not sure. But whichever, there's no doubt that between them the two have absolutely dominated eyeball time over the last many decades.

As they should. After all, what is fiction's purpose? It's to give us what we don't get in real life – the chance to live an alternate life, to see and do and feel things we otherwise wouldn't.

At the initial level, crime fiction is consolation. In real life, if your car gets nicked or your lawnmower gets stolen out of your shed, you're never going to see them again, and the police are never going to catch the guys who took them. The cops probably won't even bother to come over. You'll live with a dull buzz of frustration and a rankling sense of vague injustice.

But in a crime novel, you bet you'll get your stuff back. The thieves will be caught and punished. By the novel's end – after many hiccups along the way – order will be restored, and the feeling of frustration and injustice will be replaced by a tight-jawed smile of satisfaction. You'll get what you don't get in real life.

And more. Perhaps you'll get an illuminating analysis of why crimes happen, for what social reasons, and where, and in what circumstances. You'll meet different people, with different backgrounds and different priorities. Crime novels – perhaps by default – have become the last socially realistic genre we have. Today we read Dickens to find out what life was really like in the distant past. Who will people read a hundred years from now to find out what 2022 was really like?

Quite possibly they'll read the authors in this collection. Right now they're just starting out. Some might prosper and become famous names, with enduring titles recalled with admiration and affection. If they do, all credit to them. Their task is not easy, and success is a distant and fragile goal.

All credit to the University of East Anglia, too. It's the UK's pre-eminent writers' university, and had the guts to introduce a crime-fiction MA that treats the genre with seriousness but not preciousness. I have visited many times and have always been impressed. So enjoy the samples herein – fierce, new, original and compelling – and then put the book away. Check it again ten years from now, and see who eventually made it big. I'm sure you'll find at least one. Maybe more.

Lee Child
New York
2022

TOM BENN
Introduction

Our cohort of 2020–2022 crime writers has been tested by the fates. Denied the opportunity to first introduce themselves and their work in physical classrooms on campus, they were unable to establish a three-dimensional rapport. Instead, they suffered non-residential residentials online; international travel restrictions; the ambient anxiety of producing prose fiction for a post-truth, pandemic world.

Whether by accident or design, some of that global tumult will have bled into their work: the chosen words and white spaces between them. These crime writers have had to ask more of their genre. They have had to place greater trust in themselves and each other, as well as question the borders between past and present, victim and villain; between genres, readerships, identities. They have needed to acquire not just the tools of superior craft – voice, theme, plot, place, etc. – but superior scrutiny, supportiveness and generosity.

Lucky for you, these crime writers have persevered. Through webcam tiles, laptop keys and microphones, they have communed and considered, laboured and produced. And here are the early rewards. Skip ahead to discover for yourself. Pick any page, any passage. How they have thrived.

Some of us read or write crime fiction to *escape* personal or systemic real-world injustice, while others reach for crime fiction to *expose* these injustices, to examine and process them. Either mode can be art and/or entertainment. But words are always written and read as acts of faith and will. Reader, writer, narrator, character. Student, tutor, editor, mentor. Peer, confidant, master, apprentice. Sceptic, evangelist, champion. All fluid, interdependent words; roles that intersect, overlap, and are only conditionally occupied, despite the ceremonial magic of institutional authority governing or monetising their illusory fixity. In each of these quantum positions – positions that exist inside and outside of the moving text – you will always find somebody trying to understand, as they try to be understood. The necessary tensions between these two desires open conduits for harmonies. Righteous songs of inquiry and innovation. Of vandalism and subversion. Of conservation and cross-pollination. Of cosmic reckoning, hidden voices, stubborn truth.

Read these eleven crime writers as they each command and repurpose elements of genre to try to better understand something different, and differently. They have helped one another to deepen if not always solve the mysterious *whats*, *hows*, and *whys* essential to great crime writing. Their own dynamic, dramatic schemes of expression and escape. Narrative vessels shaped to interrogate the world.

I am so proud of what these crime writers have achieved already, and excited for all of the questions and generosity in their work to come. So much is uncertain at present, but here is proof of the future.

This eclectic anthology showcases the first 5,000 words of each novel created by the writers completing from UEA's renowned Crime Writing MA course in 2022.

A S U N   Á L V A R E Z

Asun Álvarez is a writer and translator with an interest in language, history, mythology, and general nerdery. A published poet, *Son of the Country* is her first novel. She is currently halfway through a sequel – essentially, a heist story set in Shakespeare's London and Venice, with magic.

asun@asunalvarez.com

Son of the Country
The first two chapters

CHAPTER ONE

A curse on the mother that bore you. A curse on the milk you suckled on. A curse on the cradle that rocked you.

Martín willed himself to keep his eyes on the buttermilk as he cursed inwardly, plunging into the barrel the paddle that he would much rather plunge down the throat of the bowlegged fellow who walked past, laughing at his own wit. Seán, he thought he was called, and the tenor of his jeers was obvious by now: something about Martín's manliness, or lack thereof, and doing a woman's work. As if he hadn't churned butter a thousand times, back in Asturias, and very good butter it had been.

He wondered whether an actual curse, or one of his mother's spells, would work here. But he knew better than to try, and just viciously muttered to himself, in pointless defiance, the little rhyme she had taught him as a child:

Firi tixeiru
tarabicón
saca manteiga
e lleite non

Wound, swivelling blade; draw out butter, not milk. A nursery rhyme, really, nothing remotely witchy about it – but suspicious enough coming from his mother, even more so to Castilian ears. Never say it in front of outsiders, she had warned him, and he hadn't: he had always been so careful about those things. Not that it had done either of them much good.

He quashed his frustration, staring and not quite seeing the landscape that in many ways was so similar to Asturias: red cows grazing in fields of green parted by low stone walls, and beyond them a dark tangle of woods, and, beyond those, grey hills rising out of the fog – only here they were craggier, and flat at the top like giants' tables. The late January morning was cold and grey and sunless, as all mornings had been since he had come back to consciousness on the cot behind Colm's hearth.

He'd been put to churning to unman him, that was clear. A humiliation. But he didn't mind it – it was a familiar task that took his mind off things, and most of the women here treated him kindly. Most, but not all. As with the men, there were those who resented him, who would much rather have left him and the other Spaniards shivering naked on that nightmare beach, or even handed them over to the English in exchange for some coin or some temporary goodwill. He had been told that was what happened elsewhere along the coast, where the local lord wasn't as good-hearted as Ó Ruairc and Mac Fhlannchaidh. That he was lucky, and should be grateful.

Yet gratefulness was the last thing he felt right now. He had loathed Captain Cuéllar – the only good thing about the man had been that he was a taskmaster, brutish and pig-headed enough to force-march the half-dead group of survivors through the unknown wilds. But by now Martín had mostly come to agree with his constantly referring to the Irish as 'the savages'.

He looked up, just in time to see Seán cross over to one of the nearby thatched huts that these people called houses. Seán noticed him looking and ostentatiously hawked up, spitting a gob of greenish phlegm with such thrust and accuracy that it landed, as intended, in the mud just in front of Martín's feet.

He forced his eyes back to the swirling cream.

Shipwrecked because that arsehole King Philip and his arsehole priests had refused to allow his precious Armada to be sullied by any kind of magic that might, just might, head off the storms that Elizabeth's head sorcerer was bound to send their way. Tossed, battered and bleeding, onto that hellish strand, in the midst of an elemental vortex the raging likes of which Martín had never seen before, in Spain or in the Americas. Stripped naked by whooping hordes of gold-crazed Irish villagers, as he saw his friends' dead bodies – he hoped they had been dead by then – ravaged by wild dogs. Hunted like an animal across bogland and swamps by English and Irish and *fucking marsh goblins*. Finally finding refuge with delusional, brother-murdering cattle raiders in God's idea of a joke.

And then, after fighting and defeating the English on behalf of Mac Fhlannchaidh, Captain Cuéllar and the other survivors had fled the ecstatic chieftain's tower in the middle of the night, because who in his right mind would willingly stay in this shithole unless they had to? And wounded Martín had been dumped, left, burning with fever and not expected to last the night, to die among strangers.

And now here he was. Still alive, but mangled and alone in this godforsaken sty of a village on this godforsaken island, with no way out in sight.
A curse on God.

'*A dhuine! Spáinneach!*'

Martín looked up – that much Irish he understood. Colm, his unhappy host, was calling at him from the farther end of the row of huts. He nodded towards the tower: *Mac Fhlannchaidh wants to see you.*

Colm's wife pushed him aside to take over the churn, more concerned with the butter than with her manners. He wrapped himself in the coarse dun blanket he had been given and followed Colm down the muddy path, past squawking chickens and busy women and screeching children playing in front of the village church, dedicated to saints he had never heard of, to the bank of the lake.

Colm didn't like him and was as eager to get Martín out of his house for good as Martín was eager to leave it. He had thrown a fit when he found his wife dressing Martín's wounds, with his linens off, and threatened to kick him out. And he would have done so, or worse, had Mac Fhlannchaidh not intervened. Colm must feel Martín was stealing from him: his food, his space, and most of all his peace of mind. And he was right. If the English found Martín here, they would hang all these people along with him. No wonder they resented him.

And they don't know the half of it.

It must have been nearing noon, yet a heavy, clammy mist still clung to the surface of the water, and to their clothes and faces, as they paddled across to the island. When the leather raft bumped against the rocky bank, Colm picked up the two bundles he was carrying to the tower kitchen and gestured for Martín to go ahead without him.

The island was tiny, created, they had been told, to build the thick-set, grey-stoned, moss-encrusted tower that loured above him through the fog, as if in reproach – *you still here?* He brushed his hand past the low defensive wall that stood in front of it, a makeshift parapet. He and his eight fellow Spaniards had built that wall while they held Mac Fhlannchaidh's home against the English, during those endless seventeen days and nights in December. He took an odd pride in it: they had made this, and survived.

Has it really been only a month?

Martín's leg still hurt and he limped when he walked, but he was able to climb up the steep stairs to the top floor without too much trouble, although he did have to stop to catch his breath several times. He wondered what to expect, as he hadn't seen Mac Fhlannchaidh since before the siege. The chieftain had been furious when Martín's comrades left for Scotland without warning – Mac Fhlannchaidh had hoped he would get to keep his nine highly trained Spanish guards and marry his ugly sister off to Captain Cuéllar. His hopes dashed and finding himself saddled with an invalid, Mac Fhlannchaidh had dispatched Martín out of his tower and into Colm's house as soon as his fever went down.

The chieftain was sitting at the heavy, dark table in the middle of the room, morosely picking at the remains of a meal with the tip of his knife. He was not alone. The other man, whom Martín had never seen before, was standing – tall, lean, long-legged – in front of the fireplace. Red hair. (Yet another one. It was not that unusual in Spain, of course; but the number of redheads here was ridiculous.)

Mac Fhlannchaidh glanced up as Martín came in. 'Are you looking at the women?' he barked in his ungrammatical Latin. 'I am told you have been looking at the women.'

Martín blinked. The other man turned slightly, eyeing him sideways.

'I have been put to work helping the women. I can hardly do that without looking at them. Unless you want me to cover my eyes and go around bumping into things, that is.' The red-headed man looked away again, hiding a smile. Martín added, as Mac Fhlannchaidh was frowning in dangerous irritation (his Latin, however basic, was good enough to understand Martín's back talk): 'I have not disrespected the women. Or anyone else, for that matter.'

Mac Fhlannchaidh kept frowning. He was a large, heavy-set man, his broad shoulders made even more so by the huge pelt he was wearing. He must have been in his fifties and his pale hair, which he wore long, falling veil-like down the sides of his craggy face, was turning white in places. 'There have been complaints. The men in the village say that you *Spáinneacha* pestered the women when you came along. And that *you* are now chasing after them and groping them.' He scowled, and muttered, almost inaudibly: 'And that some of them *like* it.'

Captain Cuéllar had moaned that the women here were all after him. *In his dreams, perhaps.* God, but men could be idiotic about what women did and didn't want. Dangerously so, now, though. 'Even if I did that sort of thing – which I don't – do I look like I could do much chasing right now?'

The red-headed man chuckled. Mac Fhlannchaidh glared at him, then looked Martín over, grudgingly allowing that he was indeed in no shape to pose a threat to anyone. 'Hm. Are you happy here? Has Colm been treating you well?'

'I have no complaints. And I am grateful for Colm's and your hospitality, lord Mac Fhlannchaidh. But I would like to cease to impose on your kindness and be on my way back to Spain as soon as possible.'

This was a mistake, as it obviously reminded Mac Fhlannchaidh of Captain Cuéllar, the bolting bridegroom. He stabbed at the table with his knife, trying to spear a stray crumb. 'I have troubles enough already to worry about. With the *Sasanacha*, and Ó Ruairc, and the fairy shite, and the cattle thieves, and my blacksmith gone, and next week is...' He turned to the other man, saying something in Irish that sounded like *imbolk?*

'Saint Brigid,' said the other man in Latin.

La Candelaria, Martín translated to himself. Candlemas. 'I only need some food and clothes and to be pointed in the right direction.'

'Not now,' snarled Mac Fhlannchaidh, whacking the blade hard into the table, where it stood quivering. 'Brian na Múrtha has said you are not to leave Ireland until he sends word. You will wait.'

'But...'

'I said *you will wait.*' He pulled the knife out, scowling as the blade resisted him, and grumbled in Irish about Brian na Múrtha, Brian of the Ramparts. This, Martín now knew, was Ó Ruairc, Mac Fhlannchaidh's overlord, who had extended his protection to the bedraggled fleeing Spaniards. They had never actually seen him, as Ó Ruairc seemed very busy with cattle raids up and down the country. But they had stayed with his people, and then Ó Ruairc had sent orders to the unenthusiastic Mac Fhlannchaidh to take them in. After the gaggle of Spanish soldiers had, to everyone's surprise, held his stronghold against the English by themselves, Mac Fhlannchaidh had been happier for a while. But now they were gone it was clear that he once again resented his overlord's commands. Or, possibly, his overlord altogether.

The other man turned around to face Martín. He'd be some ten years older than him, late thirties or early forties. Sharp features, with a sparse red beard. Shrewd green eyes. He looked like a fox, Martín thought, discomfited.

'It's dangerous,' the man said. 'The English have no doubt learnt of your comrades' crossing over into Scotland, and they're stepping up the search for Spanish survivors in this area. And also, other – events are under way.' He glanced at Mac Fhlannchaidh. 'This really isn't a good time. It will be easier for you when things calm down. In the summer.'

Martín was by now used to the way Latin was spoken here, Mac

Fhlannchaidh's slow, fumbling half-grasp of it having helped him to become inured to the odd local pronunciation, and to also pick up some of the Irish words that peppered his sentences. But this man's Latin wasn't halting like Mac Fhlannchaidh's – rather, it was fluent, comfortable, as if he spoke it on a regular basis.

He looked down, pursing his lips. When he looked up again, he saw that the red-haired man was watching him. Fully aware – or so it seemed to Martín – of his mutinous thoughts.

'You can read and write, yes?' Mac Fhlannchaidh asked.

'Spanish and Latin. Yes.'

'And you fought before coming here, yes? You have killed?'

Martín's jaw clenched, and this time he was certain that the red-haired man noticed. 'I am not a soldier by trade,' he replied. 'But I know how to handle a sword and a gun. As you saw for yourself.' Not that they had needed to use them much during the siege: they had just had to wait the English out while avoiding their missiles. Which Martín had signally failed to do.

'Yes, you *Spáinneacha* were good fighters,' muttered Mac Fhlannchaidh, irked again by the memory of his lost personal guard. 'Good protection. And he's an ally. Kept my castle safe while I was away in the mountains, taking care of the people and the cattle. Kept it safe from the *Sasanacha*. We need to be good hosts. When King Philip sends his people to help us fight them, *he'll know who to thank*.' He looked meaningfully at the other man, who snorted.

Mac Fhlannchaidh started saying something in Latin but quickly switched to Irish, and the red-haired man replied in kind. As Mac Fhlannchaidh grew angrier and their conversation flared up into an argument, Martín stared at the floor. The row, to judge from Mac Fhlannchaidh's frequent gesturing at Martín, was about him. And, in his experience, when people talked about him, it was never good.

The minute they take their eyes off me, I'm out of this shithole.

Martín spent the afternoon mending the fence and the rabbit hutches behind Colm's hut. It wasn't until it started to grow dark that the commotion started.

There was an outcry on the other side of the hut. He stopped to look around the corner. Seán's short, plump wife was going from house to house, hands twisting her apron, repeating the same word over and over to everyone she came across: *Niamh. Niamh. Niamh.* Niamh, judging from the growing fear in the woman's eyes, must be the little flaxen-haired girl

Martín had seen run in and out of Seán's house.

Other women gathered around Niamh's mother, then the men, drawn by the sudden agitation. Martín saw Seán as he walked home and met the unexpected tumult, the colour draining from his face when he was told what was going on. Then one of the women raised her voice above the hubbub, and said something in an authoritative tone, to the others' nods. As one, the small, clucking crowd hurried down to the churchyard, where some straggling children were still pelting each other with ice, putting off going home despite the cold.

Martín looked around. Colm and his wife had gone with the others, and now, for the first time since he had been here, all the huts around him, and the track between them, were empty. There was nobody to watch him.

He looked to his left, to where the track sloped slightly upwards and out of sight – it kept running along the edge of the lake for a while, he knew, before turning sharply towards the North. Towards Scotland, and the ships to the Spanish Netherlands there.

He slid into the empty hut, going straight for the box where Colm kept his knives. He pulled one out at random. His eyes strayed to the pallet where he knew Colm hid his purse, then thought better about it.

He stepped out again. And saw, in front of Seán's hut, the small pile of clothes left lying on the ground, next to a wooden basin, ready to be washed. The tiny linen garment on top. A child's shift.

He stared for a moment. Making sure there was no one around to see, he strode across the muddy track and reached for the dirty undergarment. Sniffed it. Then shoved it, scrunched into a ball, under his waistband.

The scent was strong and clear. Martín picked it up easily, scurrying past the backs of the houses, past the back of the church, where the little girl must have been playing before she wandered off.

The villagers were all searching along the banks of the lake, no doubt thinking that Niamh had gone down there looking for rushes – the children had been weaving odd three- and four-legged grass crosses this week, something to do with Candlemas, he assumed. But the trail led inland, towards the woods that surrounded the village, in the direction of the distant bog that he could smell from here, the loamy, rotting sweetness of peat and moss wafting in the air.

He moved at an ungainly pace across twilight fields, through the encroaching darkness that was no obstacle to his sight, following his nose. It was exhilarating to be able to run – or at least hobble – freely after such a long time on the mend, even though his thigh still hurt and the wound where the English bolt had pierced his shoulder was not yet fully healed. It was the first time he was completely alone, with no eyes watching him, he realised, since – since before he had boarded the *Lavia* in Lisbon, in May last year, actually. He was overwhelmed, for a second, by how much he had missed it.

The little girl had walked into the forest, which was surprising – one would expect folk in such a dangerous country to bring up their children under strict admonishments never to venture into the woods alone. But perhaps Niamh was slow-witted, or something unexpected had happened. Or someone, or something, had lured her away.

He heard, in the wind, the drift of several villagers' voices moving towards where he was, far behind him. They must have split up the better to search for Niamh, or someone may have seen Martín running away from the village, or both. Suddenly, he was struck cold by the realisation of the many ways in which this could go very wrong for him, and how rash he had been darting off alone on Niamh's trail like this. He had better return with the little girl alive and well, or not at all.

'Niamh!' he shouted as he followed her scent through the darkening thicket, brushing harsh leafless branches aside, the crunch of ice and frost under his feet. The air here was filled with myriad distracting sounds and smells – hunting owl, scuttling centipede, decaying stoat, the seething vegetable and animal life and death of the night forest, from treetop to undergrowth, pressing against his senses. He pulled the linen shift out of his waistband and held it to his nose. 'Niamh!'

He wandered around the woods for some time, heart sinking whenever he dropped the trail in the dark, then beating fast when he picked it up again. He was still clutching her shift when his hackles rose as the sudden, familiar *other* scent hit him. The growling that followed sounded almost like a welcome home, although he was well aware that it was far from that. He moved faster.

A small clearing. At its edge, a tiny, shivering child. And across from her, three wolves – a large, dark-collared male, flanked by two smaller females. Siblings. A small pack, hungry in the lean winter.

'*Tar anseo*,' he called out to Niamh, the Irish imperative he had heard often enough. Come here.

Niamh looked up from her paralysed fear, then started to edge towards what to her must have been just a deeper shadow in the blackness. As she approached him, her scent spiked with terror, Martín – slowly, slowly – stepped forward, placing himself between the child and the three tense, growling animals.

The male bared its teeth in a snarl, ears erect and forward, tail stiffly vertical, as Martín came closer. Ready to attack.

Without thinking, Martín bared his own fangs and growled back, ramrod straight, making himself as large as he could. It had been years since he had last done this, but the rictus came back to him as naturally as walking: the deep frown and puckered nose as he held his head high, every muscle on his face and in his body signalling dominance and threat.

The most important thing, though, was holding the wolf's gaze. And not backing down.

Martín stared into those eyes, which would likely be golden in daytime but were two glowing points in the crepuscular light. His own eyes, he knew, would look just the same. He felt the old, wild rush take over, the fierce focus of his second nature. For a moment, he forgot about the terrified child behind him, he forgot about the whispering, menacing forest that surrounded him, he forgot about the shipwreck and his wounds and the dangers and escaping and Ireland. There was only the wolf across the clearing, and the wolf that arose from within him to meet the challenge.

He didn't know how long they stood there, the other male and he, facing off. After what felt like hours, the wolf dipped his head slightly, his snarl deeper, and Martín answered by growling again and holding himself even taller. Unyielding.

A heartbeat. Then the wolf's head dropped, tail curled between his legs. Submission.

A crash among the trees behind him jolted Martín back to the clearing. Cries and torches. The three wolves immediately looked up in twitching alert, and – with one last glance of acknowledgement at Martín from the male – vanished into the bushes.

The sudden firelight and the hue and cry made Martín blink. Someone called *Niamh!* in utter relief, as if life itself had come rushing back into them, and ran to the little girl, enfolding her in an embrace.

He turned, following the father? mother? as they rushed Niamh away back to safety.

All the men were staring at him.

They stood in silence, faces still with shock in the flickering light of the torches. Then one of them, a large, burly fellow, shouted something, pointing at the little girl's shift that Martín was still holding. The man strode forward, yanked the garment from his hand, and kept shouting in Martín's face, spraying him with spittle.

Martín lowered his head and raised his hands, placating: this had happened to him before. But the large man, and the other men muttering behind him, were not appeased. They circled closer to Martín, and then the ringleader pushed him, so that Martín almost tripped back, and the others, emboldened, started shoving at him too.

He raised his arms to protect his head, hoping this would just be a ritual beating, the usual taking out of people's fears on the freak, and that they would be satisfied once they had landed a few blows.

They weren't.

The large man hit him on his wounded shoulder, hard, and Martín fell into a crouch as his knees gave way. The men closed in on him, kicking his ribs, spitting, hurling accusations and insults and curses. One of them elbowed his way through, wielding the branch that he had just wrenched off a tree. Raised it above his head to bring it down on Martín's face.

The wolf he had called up was still under Martín's skin, throbbing in his blood. He surfaced.

With the same snarl he had just used on the vanished wolf, Martín leapt to his feet, faster than his own thoughts, and snatched the branch from the man, raking the nails of his other hand across his face. Before the man could do anything but yelp, Martín had kneed him in the pit of the stomach, and bared his teeth again.

The other men came at him, furious that he had dared to turn the tables on their friend. But their fury quickly turned to alarm, then disbelief, then panic as they realised that it had been no fluke.

There were five men lying on the ground around him when the shouted order came from the trees. Martín stopped, panting, as the world slowly became human again. He looked down: his hands were red, and he tasted blood in his mouth. Not his own.

More sharp commands, which would have been unintelligible to him right now even if they hadn't been in Irish. Martín could only stand, watching and trembling, not yet fully a man again, while the aftershock of the fury ebbed from his veins.

The red-headed man from the tower briskly stepped over to the fallen men, looking down at them: from their groans, they all seemed to be breathing and at least semiconscious. The men still standing were huddled together, about to run away any second. He gave more orders, and they hurried forward, dragging their fallen comrades away as fast as they could.

He turned to Martín. 'Are you all right?' he asked. Hand on the hilt of his sword.

Martín nodded. Swallowed. Words were coming back to him, but he didn't know what to say. 'I found Niamh,' he managed to say, eventually. 'I went looking for her.'

The red-headed man bent down, picked something up from the grass. The linen shift. 'They thought you used this to attract the wolves. That you had meant to offer them the child.' He looked him in the eye. 'You followed the trail of her scent, didn't you?'

Martín swallowed again, mouth suddenly even drier.

The man tucked the shift under his belt. 'Come on,' he said. 'We need to get to the castle. I told them I'd deal with you, but I don't want to risk anyone in the village becoming hot-headed and getting bad ideas.'

They walked in silence through the forest and fields, avoiding the village, back to the bank of the lake, where they crossed over to the tower. 'Go up to the top floor and wait there. I need to talk to the chieftain,' the red-headed man told Martín. 'And wash yourself,' he added, gesturing at his own face. 'We don't want anyone dying of fright if they see you like that.'

Mac Fhlannchaidh must have retired recently for the night: the embers were still glowing in the fireplace in the main room. A pallet, an ewer and basin, and some folded linen towels had been laid out nearby, no doubt for the red-headed man. Martín picked up one of the towels and washed his hands and face, the cloth and the water that dripped back to the basin turning dark with blood.

He waited in the gloom, standing by the door, alert. He didn't think they would harm him now, here, but there was no telling what Mac Fhlannchaidh – or indeed, the red-headed man – might do after what had happened. Eventually, the man returned with two servants, one of them carrying another pallet, the other a tray that he set on the table. Once the servants were out of the room again, the man gestured for Martín to sit with him.

'It's for you. You must be hungry, after...'

He *was* ravenous. He always was, after, the wolf-rage took so much energy. The other man sat down to drink, and Martín got started with the meat they had brought. It was very good beef, but boiled and fairly insipid, the way they seemed to prefer to cook it here.

He ate in silence for a few minutes. Then the red-headed man asked: 'Have you always been... like this?'

What he meant was: *Is it a curse?* Martín swallowed another bite and replied: 'Yes.' He washed down the coarse oaten bread with what turned out to be surprisingly tolerable wine. 'I'm a *lloberu,* a wolf man. I got it from my mother, it ran in her family. I – can do some things wolves do. Smell like them, see and hear like them. I don't turn into an actual wolf, if that's what you're thinking.'

'I know,' replied the man, nodding at the goblet Martín was still holding. 'That's silver.'

Martín snorted a laugh, surprised. *Fox-like indeed.*

'You fight like a wolf, too. I've never seen anything like it.'

Martín said nothing. He took another long swig of wine.

'Can you control it?'

'Up to a point.'

'Ah.' He looked at Martín, thoughtful. 'I know some gallowglass – they are Scottish mercenaries, descended from Northmen – some gallowglass claim they are possessed by a bear spirit when they fight. But I have never seen it, myself.'

Martín moved on to the cheese. 'How did you find me? In the forest?'

'I saw you running towards the woods, and some of the villagers saw *me* follow you and ran ahead. I had gone down to Colm's because it was clear you were determined to leave. I wanted to find you before you tried to escape.'

'To stop me.'

'To give you my purse and my sword. So that at least you'd have a chance of surviving.'

Martín stared at him. Eventually, he asked, 'So what happens now?'

The red-headed man sighed. 'I came to Ros Clochair to discuss some business matters with the chieftain, but then he sprang on me that he wanted me to take you into my own household, in An Tobar, because the villagers were unhappy about you being here. I refused – nothing against you, you understand, but it's only me, my sister, and a few servants, and I didn't want to place them at risk. He was trying to bully me into taking you in, before.' He frowned. 'Now you can't stay here, not after what happened. The villagers think you are a *conriocht*, a sort of malevolent shapeshifter, or worse. They will kill you as soon as you turn your back. So it looks like you're coming with me after all.'

Martín laid the knife down on the table. 'I just want to make my way to Scotland. Or to a ship going anywhere but England.'

'As I told you before, the situation is very volatile right now. The English are hunting down and killing all the Spaniards they can find; they're afraid they will spark a rebellion. By all accounts, Elizabeth's Deputy in Ireland has had hundreds of them slaughtered already.' His face clouded over, as if with some private grief. 'In Clare, the sheriff hanged more than seventy survivors of two ships like yours. After torturing them.' He looked up and saw Martín's stricken face. 'I'm sorry. But you don't want to end up like them.'

Martín shut his eyes for a second. Saw again the wild dogs on the beach, gnawing on the boatswain's face. 'No,' he said. 'I don't.' He took a deep breath. 'I'll wait. And thank you. For your hospitality. I promise I will be a good guest. I don't want to be a burden on you or your household.'

The man smiled, a small, secretive smile that made Martín want to get up and *run*. 'Oh, if I'm right, you will prove quite useful, Martín.' He pronounced it correctly, with the stress on the last syllable. 'By the way. My name is Domhnall.'

Nina Bhadreshwar trained as a journalist in South Yorkshire before relocating to Watts, Los Angeles in the 1990s with her own magazine. She's worked in education and music journalism in England, Scotland and California. She has published poetry and non-fiction and paints murals. This is her first novel.

ninabhad@gmail.com

The Day of the Roaring

KENYA – APRIL 1955
Njambi

I can see the big Meru oak, its broad straight trunk and starred leaves, stark against the orange sky. Damp air rising like steam from the central highlands. The south-east kusi monsoon comes. The oak forest's magnificence diminished now, cut down in its prime for the grained wood. They will not grow again like this although they grow fast. The white blossom with the dark, dark mauve inside, its green fruits still ripening. I remember as a child, before I went to Kijabe, sitting with my father under the same Meru oak, the fruits black-brown ripe for picking, half-ravaged by monkeys and men. Peeling the skins off, digging with a stick in the deep loam soil, burying them in a row.

Cicadas crack the still in black-green fringed forest. River water a black Kenyan tea – not English tea, no milk. Moja, mbili, tatu, nne... I am escorted by four of the African loyalists, boys my age, some from the Catholic mission, carrying long sticks to look like rifles in the dark. Only one has an oversized rifle. He looks ridiculous. I am seeing through this blindfold. These boys cannot catch a fish or a goat, but they think they have power. This is danger. Insects screech and throb through the layers of leaves. I know we are walking into evening now. I hear the rush of whispers and the crack of footsteps over dry straw. Then warmth of a flat, dry, calloused palm on my arm.

'Jambo...aberighani?'

He speaks like I have just come on a visit. A voluntary visit. He takes me by the hand and leads me into a cool space, away from the humid kusi air, a slow drizzle pattering on corrugated iron roof. I can't see now as daylight has just about gone. There's the muffled sound of running water.

'A chair. On your right. Sit.'

I stumble over a tea chest and feel my hip hit the sharp metal corners. I grab the rough wooden rim for balance. He gently pushes me towards an empty oil drum, abrasive with rust. This is not a chair. There is a waxed cloth folded on top to act as a cushion. I try to sit on it. The rim of the drum presses against my thighs.

'Sit.'

I try to take the blindfold off.

'No. Leave it. We see you; you do not see us.'

Oh, but I do. I do see him. I see him because I can hear him. He is Atu, the sergeant who came to Miss Hulda's place, who took the body. His face is round and shiny. The whites of his eyes are yellow. He is not Kikuyu. And there are others here, standing around with their sticks. These men are boys. These confused men-boys sitting around a tea chest and old oil drums in the dark. The men-boys do not know they will come for them too.

'They are destroying Kenya. You need to tell us where he is. Ebu.'

'I have not seen my husband for many moons. I do not know where he is.'

A pause. He moves closer, circling me.

'You do.' The low whine of a mosquito, like a dying saw, circles with him, undulating over the rank air. Two shadows enter with kerosene lamps. I see silhouettes and hollows, distorted shapes. I do not see the blood on their linen, but I can smell it. Atu creaks his neck from side to side.

I feel fear like blood rising in my veins. The shadows get closer.

'Maybe you need help remembering.'

'I cannot remember what I do not know.'

He laughs. It sounds like mud in his throat and all I hear is the monotonous moan of the mosquito.

'Ah, yes. Indeed.' This is an English voice, out of the dark. I see the milky outlines, hear the hard consonants.

'They cannot remember what they do not know. If you cannot tell us what we need, there are other ways we can get at it. I am sure you do not want those. You have children?'

I stand mute. A sarcophagus. They will not know my child.

'No problem. Your children have no land. Your treachery has robbed them.'

My treachery? This is Atu, for whose family my father gave goat milk when they had nothing.

The milky man stands in front of me. I can smell his stale breath. It smells like mould on coffee.

'You are a traitor to Kenya. You are hiding the Mau Mau.'

'I am no traitor.' I will not say sir. He is no sir. There is a babbling behind me. Atu steps forward.

'The men here, some Kikuyu, tell me you are iruga. We shall soon see.'

The fear rises to my ears. I feel him take my arms. He pins them back, another lifts my skirt, another knee levers my legs apart, pushes me back on the drum.

'Eww.' The boys giggle like idiots.

'She is iruga. Even the Kikuyan men would not touch that.'

'What?' This is English man.

Atu says, 'She was raised by the Stumpf woman, sir. She wouldn't let the elders perform the cleansing ceremony.'

I won't let. I won't let. I want to scream. *This is my body. My land. I won't let. This is not yours.*

'Yet you still protect these men? Your husband is no friend of Kikuyu if he marries iruga.'

'I am protecting no one.' I spit between teeth.

I feel the weight of wood on my cheek, through my jaw. As the black flashes light, I see the English man lift his hand dismissively, muttering to Atu. I cannot hear what.

'Your husband is Kikuyu and he married iruga? Well, he must know you can enjoy with others. Traitor one way, traitor all ways.'

They just beat me last time. Beat me worse the second time. I still do not speak. This is the third. I know what happens. Milky man returns with a glowing ember. I see it. I see it. Even though I know it, I scream. They grunt. I will not speak. They do not deserve words. Animal gets animal. I smell pig oil, ash, something rotten. Their filth, their sweat, I smell everything they are. I smell death. My body will refuse it.

They leave me dumped by the oil drum on the soiled waxed cloth, bleeding, burning. I will remember what I do know. And my child – my child will never know this. I have swallowed my seed. She is hidden in the dark. I will spit my truth far, far from here.

MONDAY 30 AUGUST 2010
Bruno

Nowt down for it. No change from a fiver for two coffees. And had to wait twenty minutes in the queue at the trailer. But that's Creamfields catering. Got to do it, though. Still buzzing. Even at 9am, after two days flat out raving, Charlotte still looks fit, man.

'Here you go.'

'Cheers, babe.' Stares about her like she's just landed on another planet. Always loved that spaced-out vibe about Charlotte since I first saw her at Impy's.

'You seen Amy, Bruno? I'm getting a ride back with her.'

I shake my head. Yeah, spaced out but not ca she's from another universe. She looks at me over the rim of the coffee froth.

'How you getting back?'

'A mate.' I say.

'Maybe I can get a ride with you?'

I look at her: peachy skin, ash-blonde hair, wispy curls, pinked-up lips sucking on overpriced coffee mud with a wince, blue eyes on me but wandering off. Firefox hoodie, tight jeans, hundred-quid trainers scuffed up in mud and festival shit because she knows Daddy can get another pair just like that. Pandora charm bracelet. I imagine her stuffed in back of a Mondeo estate with greasy youts running county for Ryan, shaking blades in pocket, stuffed socks, bloodied knuckles, mouths and arseholes full of rock and H pellets. Imagine her finding it a thrill. Imagine her in a train, strung out, in a trap house. Imagine the other life she could have had at King Edward's, her getting her A level results, driving license, uni, laughing free, buzzing on someone else's shoulders, kissing someone who can give her that life. In ten seconds, I know.

'Na. Listen. Got to chip, Charlotte.'

Her face falls into the coffee. Cold, grey sludge. She tips it out on the ground, fronting like it's an accessory.

'OK. Text me, yeah?'

I look her up and down. Leave no room for hope. Push it out at ten thousand feet.

'Na. We done.'

She's not getting it, goes in for the hug. I just give her the shoulder stroke, my eyes already on Ryan's van at the far end. I let go, move through the clutter of bodies and litter through to the arse end of summer.

TUESDAY 14 SEPTEMBER 2010

A loud primal bellow. A living chainsaw rips through the forest. The day of the roaring begins as the sun, barely born, throws its orange haze over the rolling purple-green edge of the moor. Diana starts her usual morning run at 5.30am when the mists are beginning to rise off stones and bracken, diffusing into a golden spray. Summer is the last to leave the valley but up here on the banks by the woodland, where the moor edge pushes over, the season shoves in its shoulder. The lone oak stands at the door to the wild moor, arms outstretched to the elements.

She can smell the rut already.

The sweetness of a rising late summer breeze now becomes something tarter, darker and riper. Something that lingers, a pungent, ancient smell. She can't escape the earth. All things returning to their first home. The deer start their serious business here every September.

Bang! Like a starting pistol, it splits the air. The trees shudder. Silence. Two seconds. Then ravens squawk, wood pigeons flutter, ground trembles as the giant stag leaps over bracken hedge, diving deeper into the woodland.

She clutches the stone wall: damp, cold, dark. Vaults it. This is the bronze age, bracken raised like spears, the rutting season when stags stalk does, does bolt and hunters stalk stags. Predators hover. End of summer, the wanton screech of the sparrowhawk and the raucous geese squawk is a siren. No matter how knackered, even after pulling an all-nighter, the wild screams of desperate nature draw her up the path through the roots, ferns and jagged boulders. The deer dip beyond the gorse breaks, deep wooded dells, ribboned by tinkling rivulets.

Over the field, Diana swipes at her unruly black Afro curls bouncing into her eyes. *Mental note: haircut asap.* Diana's work hours and personality mean she's made few acquaintances in her neighbourhood. She really should get out more – or something. Perhaps. In twenty minutes, she will be in south-west Sheffield and her workday will swallow her whole. But here, in the fierce elemental quiet of a barely born day, nature still has first and last word.

BANG! The blast behind her rips through her eardrums, her bones. Reverbs in her head. The branch in front of her shatters, falls. She jumps to the side, all reflex now, all doe. Heart banging, she bolts across the path, the brook, stumbling on stones, green moss rush, breath hard cold knots. Don't look back. Vault the stile.

She arrives at her narrow box of a cottage, heart pumping and not because she can't run. She leans over the clematis, knowing she should stretch but she's going to retch. Her ears are ringing, her head is ringing. The shot's still ringing. Hunted. No, she can hear ringing. Real ringing. Still retching, she turns the key in the kitchen door and collapses over the oak table reaching for the phone.

'Hello?' she pants.

'Kin 'ell, lass. Who's the lucky guy?'

'Who is this?' she snaps.

'Who is this, *sir.*'

Seriously.

'Sorry, sir. Just been out...'

'Filing cabinet on the Legley Road High School site. Flies. Smells bad. Got DS Robertson going down there. Blokes can't shift the thing. The developer Geoff Thomlins's having kittens. Get down and see what's what, Walker.'

'I'm on it, sir.'

'So I gather,' he chuckles and hangs up.

On the edge of the Pennines, wild craggy boulders rear like the incisors of ancient trolls against the orange horizon. Miles of untameable yellow gorse, bracken and purpling heather hem in the Victorian sprawl of Sheffield's southwest, the city's proud corner of opulence and the barometer of success. Despite growing up in a no-nonsense northern family, she's seen it happen to the sharpest: that insidious blunting which immersion brings. The ten miles' distance into Derbyshire buys her a perspective she can't afford to lose – even if a one-bedroom cramped coal-fired cottage and no garage can be an irritation in the winter. There's a strange comfort in returning at the end of each shift, day or night, to the stoic unmoving horizon of boulders, moor, the silhouette of the stark oak snag.

The first chill of the coming winter mists up her windscreen. Sky's a darkening grey. Two hawks circle patiently.

They know.

Outside the demolished Legley Road High School, DCI Diana Walker opens the car door to the sheepish grin of Major Crimes' DS Carl Robertson. He's a tall, bulky man in his late twenties with serious blue-grey eyes and a Tintin quiff.

'I mean, it may be nowt, Boss.'

She slams the door and marches next to him, cold hands thrust deep in her blazer pockets, eyes on the blue-and-white tape manned by two uniforms. While they check her through, she pulls on latex gloves and the white suit, frowning at the barely cleared approach path.

'It doesn't smell good, Boss. CSI trying to get into the thing still.'

Diana looks up at the prehistoric skeleton of a half-demolished Victorian school. In the middle of the red-and-white taped clearing, incongruous as a lost dalek, surrounded by a vague cloud of flies, a grey filing cabinet, a 1970s Stonehenge tagged in orange paint with a splattery dub: 'Merka'. Mushroom bubble-letters.

She walks over rubble, scattered like broken concrete teeth. Robertson scrambles after her.

'Probably kids, Boss. Or some sicko put a dog in there. Summer holidays.'

Diana does a one-eighty. A group of workmen huddle around a work van on the other side of the blue-and-white tape.

'When was this place demolished?' she asks.

'Twenty-eighth July, Boss. A lot of furniture survived the demolition.'

'That filing cabinet should be in a museum.'

'The workmen think it may have been in one of the mobile classrooms and dumped here when they took them away,' Robertson says.

'But it was empty then?'

'Yes – the supervisor said they checked that no paperwork was left around. Data security or something.'

'When were mobile classrooms taken?'

'Don't know, Boss.'

'Well, find out. And check the CCTV of the site.'

Diana ducks under the tape despite the uniform's yelp. One of the workmen, obviously the youngest, stands apart nervously dragging on a roll-up. The bald ugly mug nods towards him.

'It's Sean who flipped, Detective. I think he's paranoid of filing cabinets.'

The men chuckle but Diana knows it's nerves. Sean, the young kid, built like a bull, brown-bronzed skin stretched smooth over muscles better fitted for Olympic stadiums, scowls. His shaking hand lights another cigarette.

Diana walks back over to the filing cabinet, followed by Robertson. Flies hum around the package of bin liner on the ground. She puts on gloves. Marks, the CSI lead, approaches, suited up, holding a bradawl. She takes it from him, clicks the latch of the bottom drawer. It opens with a snap, suddenly jolting out. A black cloud of flies bursts out.

Bald head buckles back, retching Greggs-pasty phlegm over his boots. Diana stands up for air but just inhales more stench. Inside the drawer, bust at its black seams, a writhing mass of white maggots feast on half a fist. To the right, eyes bubbling with larvae, the grey grimace of a head grins back from the metal tomb.

CSI Tom Marks emerges from the tent beyond the huddle of shaken, irritated workmen still slouching, smoking, squinting into the sun, alternatively answering a volley of questions from two uniforms.

Diana marches back over the rubble to Marks.

'How long?'

'Hard to tell in this heat. The foreman says place was demolished in July, but this is fresh meat. Maggots still. In this heat and a metal filing cabinet, like being in an oven on Gas Mark two. Not enough blow flies yet. I'll need to get it to the lab to be sure but...'

'Roughly?'

'Two weeks max.'

Diana looks around, scrutinising the wreckage from the 1960s: turquoise painted drainpipes and chipped rusty frames. 'No CCTV?'

'Just over there, Boss, over the whole site. Thomlins took security off after demolition,' Robertson says.

'Why was the CCTV taken down?'

The workmen shrug en masse. 'Quality Assurance or something. Boss said company was being audited for compliance with building regs and that.'

Diana frowns.

'Get details from Thomlins,' she calls over to Robertson.

'Nobody else on-site?'

'No. Like I said, there were a few bods with clipboards, vests and hard-hats. From council or auditors. Not sure. They had to check that there was no data or records left on-site.'

'They never got in our way.'

'Geoff Thomlins is not pleased. Wants to get cracking on the development.'

'Tough. He'll have to wait while we're done.' Diana shrugs and turns to walk across the rubble. Robertson swallows, chasing after her.

'Boss...' Diana stops, turns.

'I used to work here.'

Diana stares at him, incredulous.

'When?'

'2006–2007. I was a teaching assistant. It's what made me want to go into policing.'

Diana sighs, surveying the wreckage from the 1960s behemoth: rusty turquoise piping, shards of grey, frost glass, splintered yellow desk wood, etched with decades of teenage rage and obsessions – all piled on top of a pyre of concrete rubble.

'Smashing. I'll have to run it past the Super. School closed officially July, right?'

'All the years under Year 11... closed August 2009 and just Year 11s in to take GCSEs. Then it all closed in July. But they were moving the mobile units off and out earlier.'

Diana peers down the road. A black-windowed Jeep cruises past, blasting out Dizzee Rascal.

'Bit weird, innit?' remarks Robertson. 'I mean, just doesn't look right.'

'Not really what you'd expect to find in a filing cabinet, no. And most filing cabinets are not left out in the middle of a yard.' Diana looks up at the tree line. 'OK, find me everything you can. House-to-house for anything unusual the past month. I need to get an ID as soon as possible. So, give me a list of school employees, students, parents. Trawl missing persons.' She pauses, frowning. 'And I want everything about the history of this building and planning permissions.'

Diana looks at the filing cabinet's back, tagged with bright orange spray paint in huge letters, filling the entire length and breadth. 'Merka'.

'Find the tagger. Any tags around the city. Add that to the house-to-house. Any unlikely lads or lasses about. Pity CCTV was taken down. Marks, can you find out how old this paint is please?'

Marks approaches, bends, scrapes with a small tool. 'Recent – within a couple of weeks.'

'This filing cabinet's been here at least as long because the drips are on the rubble round it.'

'Most likely to be kids.'

'Maybe.' Diana's eyes root around the surrounding rubble. She nods at something five yards away. Marks goes over, picks up a battered spray-can, rattles it.

'Empty. Will take for fingerprints. Nozzle still here too.'

She wanders over the gnarled teeth of a ravaged school, shards of concrete, spears of rusty window frames.

'Moving a filing cabinet is noisy business. Even in the mud. How come no one heard this? What other noises were going on?' Diana asks the air. Robertson looks around.

'Noisier during peak times and there's been the roadworks, Boss.'

'Find out the dates of those. And if they worked overnight.'

As she walks back and forth, trying to outline the drag-route of the filing cabinet by the ruts in the mud, she sees something glisten against the crumbs of concrete. Not like the dirty shards of glass in the main yard. She stoops in gloved hands, picks up a smooth clear acrylic nail, shining like a shell on the pebbled shore, the remnants of the wrecked ship of

Legley Road High School behind her, the stark bulk of the filing cabinet cargo ahead. Diana calls over to Marks. He approaches with his ever-ready supply of plastic evidence bags.

'This.'

He stoops, frowns, pulls out tweezers and bags the nail delicately.

'Not usual for a demolition site.'

Marks gets up, nodding. 'I'd put a tenner on neither the tagger or workmen having manicures.'

WEDS 15 SEPTEMBER 2010

Diana can never find a parking spot at HQ police car park. It's always the same: rammed with cars. In ten years, she's yet to find out what game she has to play in order to secure one. Getting back to Major Crimes HQ involves finding a side street without double yellows within a five-minute walking distance to Merrick Street. She always appears last at briefings and to the office after a crime scene. They just assume she can't keep time. This afternoon, Robertson is already stationed at his desk, scrolling through a list of names on an old monitor.

'Nice one, Robertson,' says Diana. 'Staff and students, yes?' She peers over his shoulder. Robertson's desk is renowned for being orderly – unlike Diana's own which is a jumble of notepads, plastic coffee cups, bulging beige files and Post-it notes stuck on any and every surface. Robertson, on the other hand, has a potted aloe vera plant, a pen tidy, a labelled stapler and a personalised coffee mug, a gift from his fiancée, Daphne. He seems to be immune to the piss-take.

'Made some calls, Boss. Most of them out of work, on supply or at school. There's a couple who didn't appear at start of term for their new roles...'

'Oh?' Diana frowns, sitting on the corner of her desk.

'The Head of PE and Gifted and Talented – or rather ex. Leroy Young. He never showed up to his temporary contract post at High Peak. His wife says she hasn't seen him since Bank Holiday weekend.'

'And that's not odd?'

Robertson shrugs. 'She sounded more pissed off. They're separated. Said he'll be off with some new tart. She's done worrying. Just mad because he was a no show to the kid's birthday party. Not even a card.'

'Okayyy. And?'

'Yeah... another. John Daniels, the Head of School. Still not showed up to his new post as Deputy Head at Pitsmoor High. Divorced before the summer. Ex-wife says she's not been in touch since so has no idea.'

'Got any recent pics?'

Robertson clicks, brings up an image of an athletic black man.

'Leroy Young.'

'OK... not him for sure. But bookmark that.'

'I've still got six other members of staff to...'

'Let's see the Head.'

Robertson clicks on another link. Diana stares at the photo, head on one side. Frowns.

'Next of kin?'

'Not sure. There's the ex I just spoke with, but her address is different. His dad lives in a care home in Birmingham. Mum died last year of ovarian cancer.'

Diana inhales. 'Bring the ex-Mrs Daniels in.'

Diana walks into the Chief Medical Officer's office. His long, lean fingers scroll through slides on a projector.

'I've not seen anything like this in three decades. Even on conferences.'

Diana inhales sharply.

'Well, one thing's definite. It's murder you're looking at. He was killed before he was butchered. Look here...'

Diana moves round to where he's pointing at the screen. There's a clear bullet hole at the base of the neck. A large bullet-hole.

'He was shot. I would say from at least 30 yards. With a rifle.'

'A rifle?'

'Yeah. I've not seen that kind of bore. Those ballistics. But it's certainly not a handgun. And those fern spores. They're from the moors. Woodland. I don't think our Mr. Daniels was murdered near Legley Road.'

'What about the weapon for butchering?'

'Butcher knives. Meat cleaver.'

'A butcher?'

Gorman taps the screen with his pencil, shrugs. 'Or a surgeon. They knew what they were doing, that's for sure. And that mole on his cheek...'

The intercom buzzes. 'DCI Walker, Mrs Daniels is in reception.'

'Rock and roll. Let's go.'

Diana meets Mrs Joy Daniels in the foyer. She looks concerned, like she might be late for a train or has forgotten to switch the iron off despite her well-groomed appearance. Magenta nails, highlighted hair. Simple white shirt, jeans and platform sandals, clasping and unclasping the clip on her shoulder-bag. Marks and Sparks class.

She frowns. 'Do I really have to do this? I mean his dad's –'

'In a nursing home in Birmingham. With Alzheimer's.'

Mrs Daniels sits back in a sulk. 'There's his sister in Australia. Our decree absolute came through in May.'

'We just need a positive ID.'

Mrs Daniels sighs. 'Well, I know he's been out and about this summer. A mate of mine saw him at some charity party in Derbyshire. Just because he's not answering my calls means nothing – we're divorced. Not been speaking for a while.'

'His neighbours haven't seen him since the week after Bank holiday,' states Diana, checking through her notepad although she knows it for a fact.

'Probably ducking and diving his debts. As per usual.' Mrs Daniels' lips are set in a firm line of exasperation.

Diana looks at her. 'Are you alright?'

She sighs. 'Can't believe I'm doing this after everything he's put me through.'

Diana just nods; she rarely feels sorry for ex-wives.

'This way then. The Chief Medical Examiner will talk you through.'

The room's cosy, bit like Diana's old therapist's: purple curtains, green houseplants, cream cushions, an oak coffee table. Two glasses of water. A tape recorder whirs. Mrs Daniels sits on an armchair facing Diana. Gorman, tall, straight-jawed, broad shouldered, in wire-framed spectacles, enters, holding a large envelope. He half smiles. Brief introductions are made. He sits down, pulling his immaculately creased trousers up an inch from the knee.

'We are going to see just the picture of a head, no body, Mrs Daniels. As I think DCI Walker explained...'

Mrs Daniels slowly closes her eyes and ejects an angry sigh. She opens her eyes and looks directly at Gorman, poker-face.

'The remains were found in several black bin liners in a filing cabinet. There was obvious decomposition. You mentioned he has a broken nose, a scar in his cleft...'

He places a photo face down on the table. Mrs Daniels' perfectly manicured hand reaches out, flicks it over, like a card in a game of rummy. She breathes in fast, blinks. Flicks the photo back down. Her fingers tremble and she clutches her purse as if for support.

'He don't have a mole on his left cheek but... yeah. That's him. That's John.'

Gorman turns towards the tape recorder: 'For the record, Mrs Daniels, ex-wife, formally identifies the head as being that of John Daniels... Thank you, Mrs Daniels. DCI Walker will take you through to the grief counsellor.'

Mrs Daniels stands up, smoothing her shirt bodice. 'I'm OK... it's nowt to me...'

She takes two steps towards the door, stumbles, falling against the sofa. Diana catches her but she's out cold. She sighs.

'Not sure if I can say that's a positive ID. The mole...'

Gorman stands up. 'If you'd let me finish in the morgue – that was no mole. That was one very bloated tick.'

'Walker! In here.' A shiny foreheaded wedge of pink flesh framed with wisps of auburn wire appears in the glass-officed doorway.

'Wish me luck with the Super!' Diana hisses to Robertson, sliding off her desk.

Entering Detective Superintendent Marchant's office is like entering the Tardis. Medals, certificates, trophies, press clippings, a glass filing cabinet, the huge mahogany desk with a massive blotter and several beige files piled up in a neat stack. Marchant's a six-foot bulk of a man with receding auburn hair and an indelible history in South Yorkshire Police. A beat officer during the miners' strike, he's now on the threshold of a well-paid retirement. Officers say they can tell time by him. His father led the policing of the miners' strikes and Hillsborough. Retired to Spain now. Marchant's old-school South Yorkshire Police Department with all the heritage of the nefarious East and West Ridings. Diana knows he expects her to bail or ask for a transfer. She knows he hasn't a clue how to deal with her. The lads resent her status but he's under pressure from national legislature to show a more 'diverse' taskforce. Nothing too serious obviously; in fourteen more months, he'll be on the golf course every morning – not glaring from his chair at gormless policemen and pigeons.

She stands at the door. Marchant motions her to sit on the well-worn leather chair in front of his desk.

'Well?'

'Sir, it's the Head of Legley Road High School. John Daniels.'

Marchant groans, picks up the handset. 'Which line?'

'Sir. In the filing cabinet.'

He drops the handset, knuckles on forehead.

Julia Bordin has degrees in Law and Creative Writing. On her YouTube channel she discusses reading and writing. Her passion for crime fiction terrifies her friends and family, but truthfully, she writes to escape her own fears. She has two short stories published in Brazilian anthologies and *The Box* is her first novel.

juliafbordin@gmail.com

The Box
The opening of a psychological thriller

PROLOGUE

'Open up.'

When he refused, she poured boiling water on his groin. When he tried to scream, she served him the scalding egg, fresh out of the boiling pan. It instantly burned his entire mouth, but he could not scream or spit it out; she'd tied his hands and sealed his mouth with a piece of silver tape.

'This is a test,' she said, 'you're mean to me and I'm mean to you. Let's see who wins.'

He was 12 years old. As the egg burned through his tongue and palate, his silent tears ran down his face, hot with rage rather than with pain. As hot as the egg.

It reminded him of the heat inside his old house, when the fire licked the walls and ceiling, burning his parents alive.

His memory of that day is orange and loud with their screams for help.

—

CONRADO

I see you.
Everywhere you go.
I see you.
Now that a new game has begun, I can't stop it. And I'll win. I always do.
You'll see.

ALICE

February 21st, 2014.

It was the last day Alice saw Sara.

It's been over four years already since Sara went missing. Alice wakes up thinking about her cousin. She'd dreamt about Sara again, but she doesn't remember the details of the dream.

She can't help but blame herself for what happened to Sara. All the *what ifs* and *whys* keep haunting Alice. What if Alice had said she was busy that day? Why didn't she say they should go back to her place, or *any* other place in the city but that coffee shop?

She remembers the day as if it happened today.

The streets are busy with cars and people walking around, getting in and out of buses, in and out of apartment buildings, in and out of stores. Wearing sunglasses and headphones looks like a rule of attire around this part of the city, close to the university. Alice is waiting in line for the cashier at the stationery shop, buying some pencils, Post-it pads, and an external hard drive.

The girl in front of her pays for her colorful and glittery pens and three notebooks with childish flowers on the covers, all same style only different colors. Alice's guess is that the girl just got out of high school, but high school hasn't left her yet. By the final year of college, she'll carry a notepad and a single pen if she's lucky to remember it. Everyone is excited and dedicated at the start of college, and either don't care anymore or are eager to leave by the end. Alice has been through that phase of life already.

She pays for her things and leaves the store stashing her new items in her grey eco-bag. It is so hot she thinks Hell just opened its gates to welcome everyone. She should have put on a dress, maybe shorts. It takes a minute for her to realise her phone is ringing. It takes a while for her to find it because she always carries too many unnecessary things in her purse. And the phone keeps on ringing.

'Hey! Watch out, you bitch!' A man shouts right at her ear when she accidentally bumps into him trying to find the stupid phone.

'Wow, rude. I'm sorry, didn't see —'

'I don't fucking care, are you blind?'

'What the fuck? I'm sorry,' she says. She gets away from him and he's still cursing at her. 'Dick,' she says to herself. He looks like a normal person, jeans, t-shirt and a cap, but he's taller than Alice, so she won't mess with him. He stares at her for a second too long and she feels a cold rush in her body, even with the hot sun over her head. The phone is no longer ringing. She hopes it wasn't her project manager. The deadline is still 3 days away.

She crosses the street and her phone rings again. On the second ring she picks up. It's Sara.

'Oi linda!' sounds the candy tone of Sara's voice. 'Where are you right now?'

'Hi, I'm close to the university campus,' Alice replies. 'I came to that big stationery store they have here close by. Why?'

'It's my day off and I'm meeting with Mariana later for dinner, but I have some time to kill. Are you free right now?'

'Oh, so I'm your time-to-kill-option, is that right?' Alice smiles.

'Don't be jealous, Cuz.'

'What about we meet at the coffee shop near campus, is that okay? I was just heading there for an iced coffee anyway.'

'Great! But it'll take me about fifteen to get there,' Sara says.

'That's okay, I can wait. I have a book with me,' Alice says.

'Why am I not surprised?' Sara laughs. 'See you soon, love you.'

It takes Alice five minutes to get to the coffee shop and it's crowded, but there's air conditioning and it's a relief against the hot atmosphere outside. Three people with backpacks and tired faces stand up and free a small table by the corner which Alice is quick to grab before anyone else sees it. She puts her heavy purse and eco-bag aside and grabs her Kindle. She just bought *The Cuckoo's Calling* by Robert Galbraith and is excited to see what all the fuss is about, other than it being a pseudonym for J.K. Rowling, of course. She just hopes there's a good detective and a great, crazy antagonist.

She's startled when the largest cup of iced coffee is put in front of her. She's still a bit shaken up from that guy from earlier. To lighten the mood, with the coffee comes the biggest smile on Sara's face when she sees Alice. Since they were kids, Sara has always been the one with the brightest light in the family. They hug and Sara sits in front of Alice with an iced coffee for her as well.

'So, what is the book of the week, you nerd?'

When they leave, an hour or so later, they decide to share a cab since Sara wants to stop at the mall on the way to Alice's. The second Alice closes the car door, she feels that cold rush again. The same guy from earlier is still there. He's looking straight at them. Alice mentions him to Sara on the ride, but she says that Alice shouldn't make a big deal out of this, that it's nothing, that he is probably just waiting for someone. Since they are away from him, Alice lets it go. Sara is probably right, and Alice is just overreacting again.

Alice is on her phone doing God knows what when the car stops in front of the mall.

'I'll call you tomorrow, Ali. Love you.'

'Okay, bye!' Alice says without taking her eyes off the phone.

That was the last thing Alice said to her cousin. To this day, years later, she wonders why she hadn't told Sara that she loved her too? She's her cousin and best friend. Alice had a shrink who told her she shouldn't worry about it, Sara obviously knew that Alice loved her. Alice herself *knows* she knew it, but that doesn't make up for the fact that it was not the last thing she heard Alice saying. And she hates herself for it sometimes.

VICTIM#1.REC

What the heck?! Where am I? HEYYYY, IS ANYBODY THERE?

[heavy panting and muffled moans]

Ouch, my neck hurts.

My name is Camila. Camila Fontes Cedro. I'm 22. I'm a student at Cornelius South. I'm a first-year med student. I was walking behind the campus, and I know my mama said not to walk on empty streets at night, but how was I supposed to get home? I only went to the pet store to get food for Mia, my cat.

[gasp]

Oh my God, Mia! Is she okay? Has someone remembered to go my place and get her? My mom hates cats, but she'd keep her safe until they find me, right?

Right???

Does—

Does anybody know I'm not there?

SOFIA.REC

Hi, it's me again, hmm, Sofia. So, I made a decision. I decided to kindly name this shithole The Box. It certainly looks like one and I won't just remind myself every day that this is my place of captivity. The walls have the bleh grey color of concrete. The mattress is thin, but he brings a change of sheets pretty often so it's always clean where I sleep. The stairs are also made of concrete, but the angles aren't sharp, they look like they have been filed to be rounded as much as it is possible. I have just realised that it looks like long bubbles or a weird cloud. The only other attraction in here is the chained bathroom door. It's so boring sometimes that I keep counting and trying to name the three-hundred and fifty-four chain links. I feel like an animal trapped in a cage and it sounds a little bit better when I rename it, so why not? In here it's just me and my sometimes really loud thoughts, the sad face I scratched on the wall with my last strong nail to pretend that I'm actually talking to someone, and not him on the other side of that door. I might not go completely mad if I pretend to be talking to a friend here.

Ha, who am I kidding? I'm not so stupid as to think he won't do the same to me as he did to the others. Someday the next girl will be hearing my recordings as well as I'm hearing someone else's through the sound system on the ceiling. The last one was Camila, she was the first to say her name so I'm holding on to her.

The sad face has a name now.

So, I guess we should get this out of the way already. I didn't want to talk about it at first, but there's no way I'll handle this if I don't talk about it to someone. I don't know. He does awful things to me here. I hate the R word, but I know it's what happens to me practically on a daily basis down here. Sometimes more than once. I'm always disgusted and afraid, and it hurts, but if I refuse, I know the consequences are worse. Nowadays I try to think of it as a job I really don't want to do but I have to get it done sooner rather than later. It's stupid, I know.

I resisted a lot in the beginning, but now I'm kind of used to it. If it's somehow possible to get used to a situation like this. The thing is that I know what will happen most of the time and if he is happy, I don't get hurt so bad. The rib I think he broke a while ago doesn't hurt as much now; it might have healed. Oh, and the neck scar has completely healed. Finally. It took too long.

Hey, I might as well take something out of this.

CONRADO.REC

Hello. Listen carefully, I'll only play this once.

First of all, you will obey my rules. It's very simple, really. To answer your question: yes, you were kidnapped and I'm the one who brought you here. There's nothing you can do about it now, so settle in. The game is about to begin. You girls teach me a lot too, so I hope I can learn a few new things with you to improve the next one's experience.

First rule, or warning, if you wish. There's a rather large dressing on the wound by your neck. Do not touch or remove it. I put it there. There's a recording device installed in you now because you'll talk about your experience in here. You can talk about anything you want, really. But you won't be silent.

This is my only demand. Just talk. Simple, right? The device self-charges with the vibration of your voice, so if you don't talk regularly, I'll make you charge it by screaming. Nobody wants that, okay? I don't even have to mention that if you manage to take it out from under your skin, I'll put it back when you're awake in the worst way possible for you. You need to think about whether you want to find out. Let's hope you won't.

There was only one girl before you that was stupid enough to test me, and I had to wait for her to wake up a few times so I could finish the procedure. Not nice for her, I'm sure.

So, let me introduce myself. My name is Conrado, we'll meet each other properly later today. I expect you to be prepared and act like a lady. Here's what will happen from now on: whenever I come down there, you will hear the door being unbolted. It's hard to miss, it makes a lot of noise. You should be expecting me quietly sitting on your bed. And the bed should always be placed right across from the stairs, where I can see it first thing. Don't move it, I get mad. If you break the rules, I'll have to do something about it. I'll bring you food, and there's water for you to drink in a little tube coming out of the wall, to the side of the bed. You can barely see it, but it's there and there's always fresh water. You just push the little button on top of it, and there you go. You'll probably have to kneel to drink.

There's another door, you might have noticed this already. It's the bathroom, but it's locked as well. You see, I can't take any chances, so whenever you want to take a shower or use the facilities and I'm not down there, you let me know. How, you ask?

Can you see a red button on the wall close to the stairs? It's like a call button in a hospital. You just press it and when I see the light upstairs, I'll come down to help you. You wait for me and then you can use the toilet.

When I get enough trust in you, you'll be rewarded. That means we can go outside for a while and you can feel the fresh air. You'll be surprised how precious this is, so don't fuck it up.

How do you earn my trust, you ask? You'll do everything I say just as I say it. You'll eat your food and shower regularly, under my watch of course. You won't break or destroy anything in there, not that there's much to destroy. And you'll make yourself ready for me whenever we meet.

See? Simple rules, right?

Oh and of course, you can scream all you want, it won't make a difference. But remember to save your voice for the recordings, otherwise we'll start on the wrong foot and you don't want that.

Be a good girl and you'll be fine. How well you're taken care of is totally up

to you. And I can be very mean if I need to be. I've been practicing all my life.
I'll see you soon. Bye bye.

ALICE

Alice and Guard, her rescue dog, are going back home from a run at the park and there are a lot of people waiting for the light to turn green so that they can cross the road. She stands at the back with Guard because he doesn't like being surrounded by too many people at once, and people on the streets are usually afraid of him because of how big he is. He really is a sweetheart to her, grateful that he has a loving home after God knows how long of a lonely life in the shelter. He looks like a mix between a German Shepherd and something else, bigger, and that's probably why he wasn't adopted before. People want cute, small and kid-friendly dogs, not dogs that look like they might kill someone just by barking at them. And that's the exact reason Alice decided to take him. Nobody would ever mess with her with Guard by her side.

While they wait for the light to change, he starts growling, the leash vibrates with his tenseness and Alice is on high alert. She notices a man standing near them. Too near for her liking. The man is looking at Guard, not at Alice, but she still feels some sort of bad vibe from the guy, like he could be nasty even to a puppy.

'What's his name?' he asks Alice with his gaze still fixed on her dog. She feels Guard's growling, but the man doesn't seem to notice it.

Alice holds the leash tighter.

'Guard, but be careful, he really doesn't like people so close to him.'

'Oh, that's okay, I love big dogs,' he says as if that cancels the warning Alice just gave. She takes a small step to the side, just in case. But the man continues:

'If I didn't work as much and weren't stuck all day at the computer shop right around the corner, I would get a big dog too.' Alice just gives him a small and uncomfortable smile and looks at the light. It's still red. It must be broken. She hopes he stops talking because she really doesn't care. But he goes on:

'If you ever need your computer fixed, come by.'

'Yeah, sure, thanks.' Why doesn't this light turn green for fuck's sake?

'Can I pet him?' As he says that, he is already too close to Guard and Alice pulls the leash just in time. Guard barks and growls hard at the same time he goes for the guy's hand. He pulls his hand away and all of this happens in a second. Alice's shoulder pinches with the dog's strength, but she manages to hold him.

'What the fuck, woman?! You need to muzzle this fucking dog! He almost bit my hand off!'

The light finally turns green for pedestrians.

'I warned you.' Alice pulls Guard and they run across the road.

By the middle of the next block, she stops to pet Guard's head.

'Good boy.'

SOFIA.REC

The nightmares still happen often. Some are so bad sometimes that I wake up shaking. Usually, alone.

There was this one time I remember he had beaten me so hard for crushing a metal mug – not on purpose, I'm not that dumb anymore. I just fell on it – and I woke up, I don't know how many hours or days later shaking and almost out of breath.

But when I realised what was going on, he was almost finished on top of me, and I just pretended I was still out so he did all the work and I didn't have to do anything else.

If it happened other times, I didn't wake up before he was done and was out of here.

ALICE

Alice wakes up in a panic. Like when people dream they are falling and wake up at the exact moment they are going to hit the ground. She wakes up to realise it was just a bad dream. Guard wakes up with her, and at a slow pace he moves towards her on the bed and licks her arm.

The arm.

She suddenly realises why she was so scared, and it wasn't because she was falling from a great height. She was pushed over.

The man that pushed her was the creepy guy from the street the other day. She is sure of it. But what really scared her was the mark she saw on his arm. She saw it in her dream when she was trying to fight for her life. She only saw the mark. It's the same pink mark she remembers seeing on the guy that was looking at her and Sara *That Day*. The day Sara went missing. Alice mentioned it to the police when she told them about the guy, but they never found any clues. They didn't even try. That's how she feels because her cousin is still missing.

That man that Alice and Guard have encountered in the corner of the street the other day must be him.

Is it him? What if it is? Alice is confused and scared and angry. She didn't pay much attention to him when Guard almost bit off a piece of him. Maybe he did have a mark on his arm, but she doesn't remember seeing it.

What she does remember is the feeling she had while she was close to him. A cold sensation down her spine, as if something was really wrong. Like he was mean, even though he didn't say anything mean to her. Guard must have felt that too, otherwise he wouldn't have attacked.

Alice needs to find out if this is the same guy that took Sara. But how?

He didn't tell her his name, or she didn't pay attention because she just wanted to get away from him. But he did say he worked at the computer shop near there.

That's it. She can find his workplace and from there she will find this son of a bitch and figure out what's happened with her cousin since the police haven't done anything about it.

At this point, four years after, Alice doesn't know if she wants Sara to be found or if she wishes for her cousin not to be suffering anymore. It nearly kills Alice, just thinking about it.

CONRADO

You are so hot to watch, Clara. But I think you know that. And you like it.

I remember the first time we met. You were desperate and I was the only one who could help you.

I was in the back of the store, dealing with a broken keyboard – and how the hell do people break a computer keyboard? I have no idea – and I just heard the banging on the glass door like it was made of concrete.

You wanted attention, that's okay.

I put on my best professional but kind face and unlocked the door. Your smile of relief lit up the room. And that's when I decided you would be the next player in my little game. You knew what you wanted, but you needed someone to help you get there.

'Thank God you guys are open!' you said. You entered the shop past me while I was still holding the door. 'I need my computer fixed, like yesterday.'

'Everybody needs something for yesterday, I'm afraid,' I said. I wanted to see how far you would go with that attitude.

'Well, I have a paper due the day after tomorrow and this fucking screen went black out of nowhere!'

'Okay, let's see what I can do for you.'

I saw that you were impatient and frustrated, but that didn't change things. It just made things easier for me.

'Yeah, sorry, this will take a while,' I said.

You frowned and started going through your purse.

'How much?'

'I'm sorry?' I said.

'How much do you need for this *not* to take a while? I'll pay double your fee if you need, but I need this computer working.'

'Okay, calm down, that's not how things work. But I want to help you, miss...?'

'Clara, sorry.'

'Pleasure to meet you, Clara, I'm Conrado.' I didn't offer my hand for a shake and you didn't look like you were expecting a proper introduction. 'I assume you don't have another one you can use to finish your paper?'

'You think, Sherlock?' you said and as soon as you said it your expression softened. 'I'm sorry, today isn't going well.'

'That's okay. Look, here's what I can do for you,' I said with a plan already in mind. 'I can lend you a used computer that is a little bit older than yours but works perfectly.'

'Oh my God, seriously? Thank you, I love you already!' You almost hugged me, I could see, but you changed your mind in the last second.

'It's fine,' I said, 'I just need all your contact information, please.'

Everything I asked you gave me. Full name, age, social security number, but when I requested your address, you hesitated.

'You really need my address?'

'Sorry, yes,' I said, 'it's just company policy because you get to keep one of our computers for a while.'

With that last bit of information, I had everything I needed to get started on you and our little game, and you left happily with my special computer. I could do the rest when you turned it on later that day.

And I did.

It's 5:30 am. Earlier than Alice's usual wakeup time. She couldn't sleep because the thought that this could be the guy who took Sara didn't leave her mind all night. She dreamed about him again. Yesterday it was raining too hard for her to go out looking for the computer shop he'd mentioned. Guard gets agitated in the rain. As big as he is, he's afraid of storms and loud noises. But today is a different day.

Alice looks out the window and even though the sun isn't up yet, she can see the sky is cloudy. No rain yet, but she wants to wait for the sun to show up before taking Guard on the exploratory walk, so they still have a least one hour until it's light outside. It will still be too early in the day to be walking around the streets with all the stores still closed, but lots of people go running or walking their dogs before leaving for work. Alice will blend in perfectly with those few courageous souls who get up with the sun for the sole purpose of exercising. She does love running, but never this early. She likes her bed too much for that.

She makes herself a big mug of coffee. Black, no sugar. She read somewhere that people who drink their coffee plain and black are more likely to be psychopaths. It's a strange thing to think about, but she wonders how an actual psychopath would like their coffee. Thinking about it and what she's about to do, she leaves her coffee about halfway full and almost cold. She's too agitated and caffeine isn't helping. The waiting is as painful as it is a relief for her. She's anxious and scared. What will she find once she figures out who he is? What will she do? What if he is crazy? Dangerous? What if he is innocent? That would be worse, for sure. Her hopes of finding something that gets her closer to Sara are already up.

Leash on. Shoes on. Hair tied. Swiss pocketknife in her the pocket of her leggings, but no music on her phone. Ever since Alice adopted Guard, she feels safe running with music on, because he can be her ears to the outside world while they are running. But today is different. They are on a mission.

So early in the morning it smells like cold as soon as she steps outside. This wet and cool wooden smell with a bit of white fog will always be her favorite scent.

The cool breeze feels amazing as it touches her skin and her anxiety calms down a bit when they pick up the pace. It's good to try and disperse both her energy and Guard's running up until that corner where they encountered the creepy man. Alice has no idea what she'll do when she finds him though.

If he is the guy, he will answer for what he did to Sara and her family. Alice is sure of that.

A few minutes later they come up to that same corner on the street. The traffic light this time is green for them, and there are barely any cars on the streets at this time of day.

Alice doesn't know in which direction the computer store is, so she decides they should walk around all the blocks a couple of streets in each way. About half an hour later and almost giving up, they go around one corner and Alice stops abruptly. Guard tugs at the lead. Alice's shoulder hurts, but she ignores it.

There. In the middle of the block across the street. She's found it.

Costa Computers
Let's solve all your problems

There's a phone number. She grabs her phone from the jacket pocket and takes a zoomed-in picture of the digits and the sign showing the name. She knows the address now. Acácia Street, 251.

'Hey boy, let's go home, okay?' Her voice is a bit shaky, but only Guard is there to hear, and he won't judge. They go around a few more blocks before heading home. She needs to run. Fast. Away. Faster.

After showering, with a hot cup of tea and no coffee by her side, Alice turns on her computer and searches for Costa Computers on the National Company Database. There. Other than the name of the owner, there isn't much more information that tells her anything useful. It's after 8:30 am, so they should be open by now.

The phone rings three times before someone answers.

'Hello? Costa Computers, good morning.' The voice is strong and sure, not shaky like Alice's. She is pretty sure it's the guy from the other day.

'Hi, good morning. Do you fix printers there, by any chance?'

'Sure. Can you bring it over here so I can take a look?' He sounds professional to her, not like a creepy person. But what does she know at this point? 'Do you know where the shop is?' he asks.

'Yes, sure. I know where it is, yeah. Who am I speaking to, please?'

'This is Conrado.'

Joanne Green is a Personal Assistant who has worked in industries including education, PR, motorsport and various departments across Northamptonshire and Thames Valley Police Forces. She is a former Coroner's Officer and uses that experience to plan how she might get away with murder. *Mummy's Boy* is her first novel.

joannegreen13@yahoo.com

Mummy's Boy
The opening of a novel

CHAPTER ONE

DS Harriet Chapman took another deep breath and folded her hands in her lap under the table. She didn't want the tremble in her fingers to give away her fears to those gathered.

She sat poker straight and looked ahead of her, her eyes catching on the cuff of ACC Lucas Cavendish's shirt, poking out from the sleeve of his jacket. He was always impeccably dressed, but today there was a button missing and a tiny forlorn thread was wobbling back and forth as he spoke.

'As you are aware, DS Chapman, we are here to discuss an allegation of gross misconduct that has been made against you.'

Harry felt sick as she listened to details of the charges being read out.

She'd been accused of providing her brother, Patrick, with an alibi. He'd been spotted frequently outside their father's house – too frequently.

After someone spray-painted 'nonce' on the side of their father's car, he was the obvious suspect. Harry had heard the call come in over the radio and had instantly formulated her plan.

Patrick was homeless but she was listed as his next of kin, so when her colleagues came looking for him, she said he'd been with her.

The next day she'd been in the CCTV suite reviewing evidence for a case she was working. By a stroke of luck, the officer beside her was looking at Patrick's case, not realising who Harry was. When the officer left the room to take a call, Harry deleted the CCTV file the officer had been looking at. They didn't know she'd done that. Not yet. And she didn't think the officer who left the room would fess-up to leaving evidence unattended. It didn't matter anyway. The next-door neighbour had a camera doorbell and it had caught everything. The spray-painting and the watching.

Patrick had been keeping an eye on Nigel. Stalking they were calling it. Protection was what it really was. Protection for Nigel's new family. And that was what Harry would do for Patrick. Even if it meant losing her job. She'd always looked out for him, kept him safe. Even when they were children. She couldn't, wouldn't, stop now.

She shouldn't have done it, but she also knew that if it came down to it, she'd do it again.

She was worried, though. It was no secret that the ACC didn't like her. He always made her working life difficult, and she knew he'd relish any chance to rid himself of the thorn she'd become in his side.

Harry really didn't want to lose her job.

If she wasn't there, who would look after the victims? No one cared about the vulnerable like she did. No one. For her colleagues, the thrill of the job was locking away the bad guys. That was part of it for Harry, too. It was secondary, though, to making sure the public didn't just *feel* safe but *were* safe.

The ACC was still talking. 'The complaint has been referred to the IOPC and they will be investigating alongside our Professional Standards Department. While the investigation is ongoing you will be suspended from all duties. You will receive full pay and benefits. The suspension will last until the conclusion of the investigation. As I'm sure you will already have guessed, your promotion to DI will be withdrawn...'

He paused for full effect.

'...regardless of the outcome of the investigation.'

Harry's stomach lurched at this revelation, even though she had anticipated it might be the case. However, nothing in her expression had given away her disappointment at this news. Her childhood had been excellent training in hiding her emotions, so she was sure the others around the table wouldn't have realised how much the situation bothered her.

'I don't need to tell you, Harry, that this is a very serious allegation.' Cavendish's voice softened a little, and the use of her first name told Harry the formalities had been dealt with and the meeting was nearing the end.

'It could result in your dismissal. You do realise that, don't you?'

Normally the ACC's voice was sharp and abrupt when talking to Harry; his kindness unnerved her. She said nothing.

'We are all aware of the circumstances and none of us are happy that your father is back on the streets. It was a... terrible business.'

Terrible didn't go anywhere near describing the pain Harry and her bother endured both before and after their father had murdered their mum. Harry's jaw tightened at the comment and the ACC coloured slightly, perhaps realising his words were inadequate.

A voice cut into the awkward atmosphere. 'I'll be leading the investigation on behalf of the IOPC.'

Harry looked towards the woman who had spoken, Susan Tremain.

'You have an impeccable record and I have no doubt we can deal with this matter swiftly. I will ask ACC Cavendish to appoint someone from Professional Standards and we'll work as efficiently as possible. I'm sure we'll have this wrapped up in no time. Clearly there are extenuating circumstances. In the intervening period, we would ask you to have as little contact as possible with those involved in the case.'

Harry had no intention of staying away from her brother. She didn't know where he was – he moved from place to place, drifting, unable to settle. He'd distanced himself after recent allegations, but she knew he would still be close, keeping an eye on their father, making sure he wasn't up to his old tricks. She would have no problem staying away from Nigel, though. As far as she was concerned, he was dead to her.

'If that's all?' Harry rose from her seat. The decision was made, no point hanging around.

'Sit down until you're formally dismissed.' ACC Cavendish hissed the words at Harry, a drop of spit landing on the table between them. Any trace of his previous kindness disappeared.

Harry didn't sit. Sitting wasn't going to change her situation and she wanted to get out of the stuffy room and uncomfortable uniform and into her jeans for a muddy walk in the woods with Cal, her large, scruffy German Shepherd.

Anyway, what was he going to do if she didn't sit? Fire her? She allowed herself a little smirk.

'I'm glad you're finding the situation amusing, DS Chapman.' Cavendish was back to the formalities. It didn't take long. It never did.

She was already on his wrong side and had been since before she'd even joined the force. She didn't much care about that. She did care about losing her job. She wouldn't show the ACC that of course.

'Sir, with the greatest of respect, I won't be sitting down. I've listened to everything you have to say. I understand, and now I'll be leaving. Thank you all for your time.' Harry nodded in the general direction of the others sat at the table and turned towards the door.

The ACC's voice sounded behind her. 'Usually, sentences that start that way imply no respect at all.'

Harry didn't turn back, she merely gave a slight shrug of the shoulders and headed out of the door.

Harry was escorted to her office to collect her belongings, and as she reached the room she shared with the rest of her team, the hubbub from within fell quiet. Just for a moment, until DC Ahmed Best broke the tension.

'Here she comes, our very own Dirty Harry!'

Christ, Harry thought. That'll be the headline when the local press get hold of this. She supposed it would go nicely beside the most recent one about her father:

Doctor Death. Local GP jailed for killing wife to wear ankle tag on his release.

The noise in the office resumed as Ahmed wandered over and gave Harry a hug, said he had no doubt she'd be back soon. She was grateful for that. The rest of the team followed his cue and they took turns wishing her well. DS Aiden Kidd was on the phone, but he motioned that he would call her later.

Aiden, his wife Tilly, and their children were the only reason Harry ever ate properly. They regularly invited her to dinner. Without them, she would definitely starve. She wasn't sure that she was feeling particularly sociable at the moment though, and she already knew she would be ignoring his calls.

As Harry lifted her small box of personal belongings, she saw movement in the corner of her eye and glanced across to see DCI Bob Duckett leaning against the doorway to his separate office in the corner of the room, a small smile playing at the edge of his mouth. The team had affectionately called the tiny office the broom cupboard until recently, and a sign to that effect had been stuck on the door. The first thing Bob had done when he'd moved in was take it down. Now there were only greasy marks where the Blu-Tack had once been.

Bob wasn't Harry's biggest fan. He was a huge fan of Cavendish, though. They'd joined Northamptonshire Police together as young men. Cavendish rose quicky through the ranks but never forgot his old friend, who could always be found trailing two steps behind. No doubt Cavendish had shared his views on Harry, and Bob was too much of a follower to have his own opinion.

Harry knew Bob would be straight round to Cavendish's office to celebrate the moment she left the building.

—

As soon as Harry reached the sanctuary of home, she stripped off her dress uniform and threw on her jeans, jumper and boots – the uniform she preferred when she wasn't at work.

She allowed herself a brief moment of self-pity. She hung her head and a lone tear dribbled down her cheek. She wasn't quite sure how she'd survive if she didn't have her job. It was the only thing that got her out of bed every day.

A wet nose nudged Harry's hand. The other thing she got out of bed for and another police outcast. Cal.

'C'mon, boy,' she said, grabbing his lead from a hook by the back door. 'Let's go get muddy.'

CHAPTER TWO

The next few days of Harry's life became a routine of getting up early after sleeping badly, sitting on the sofa flicking from channel to channel on the TV but not actually watching anything, avoiding Aiden's phone calls and taking Cal for long walks to their regular haunts.

Today was Tuesday, which meant one of their favourite places, St. Barnabas Lake.

The air was warm with a gentle breeze rustling through the trees and the lake was glittering where it reflected the early-morning sunshine. The combination of sun and dappled shade created a magical glow on the water that Harry knew on any other day would be green and murky.

She and Cal walked slowly, following the path and listening to the chatter of the ducks calling to each other from one bank to another. It was still quite early, and the only other people out were joggers, cyclists and parents of energetic toddlers who had no doubt been up so long they already felt like it was lunchtime.

Harry watched as Cal made his way to the water's edge and laughed as he ran from a flock of geese whose toddler-thrown bread he'd thought about stealing, until they spread their wings and gave a collective hoot.

'This is why you're no longer a police dog,' she said as she fished one of his treats from her pocket.

'I'm with the dog. Geese are scary.' Harry looked over to see a Lycra-clad woman smiling at her and stretching a hamstring against the back of one of the benches.

As she spoke, she leaned forwards, resting her slim body along her leg, her blonde ponytail brushing her ankle. 'It's why I like to run. I need to be able to make a quick exit when those beasts come anywhere close. They hunt in packs!'

Harry grinned. 'Unless you're dressed as a giant loaf of bread, I think you'll be fine.'

Both the woman and Cal looked dubiously towards the lake.

'I'm Cassie, by the way.' The woman held out her hand for Harry to shake. It felt slim and cool in Harry's and she wondered how this woman, who had obviously been running around the lake, looked so fresh and clean, while Harry was already feeling sticky and a little grubby. She must be warming up rather than cooling down. Harry wished she'd wiped her palm against her jeans before touching her.

'I'm Harry. And this is Cal.'

'I've seen you here before,' said Cassie. 'I'm here all the time. I like to run.' She motioned at her outfit, which looked to Harry more like clothes to pose in front of the mirror at the gym rather than something to get hot and sweaty in. But what did she know? She hated running. Walking with Cal was Harry's favourite exercise. It was like meditation. There was the ground beneath her feet, the sky above her head and her best friend at her side. Everything else disappeared. It was the only time she felt true peace.

'I've just finished, actually,' Cassie said. Well, that answers that, thought Harry.

'I normally like to round off with a walking lap before heading home. It helps bring the heart rate back down. Would you mind if I joined you?'

Harry did mind. She'd been enjoying the solitude, but Cassie seemed pleasant enough and she didn't want to appear rude. Anyway, a bit of company might be nice for a change. She hesitated only slightly before answering.

'Sure. It would be nice to have someone other than the dog to talk to.'

Cassie smiled her thanks and they set off walking in companiable silence around the edge of the water.

After a few minutes Cassie spoke somewhat hesitantly. 'Actually, I'm glad I bumped into you today.'

Harry's hackles started to rise. *Oh no, here we go.*

'Are you a journalist? I've got absolutely nothing to say to you.'

'No! No, it's not that at all. It's—'

'Ah, so my father sent you, did he? Well, you can piss right off. I've got *nothing* to say to you, or that man.'

Harry turned and stormed away, calling Cal as she went.

'You misunderstand.' Cassie called after her. 'I'm not a journalist and I don't know your dad.'

Harry kept walking and she heard Cassie following closely behind. 'I've been looking for an excuse. To talk to you. I'm wondering if you can... help me with something.'

Harry groaned inwardly. No, absolutely no way. She didn't want to help her. She just wanted a quiet walk with her dog then to go home and feel sorry for herself.

She exhaled loudly and stopped walking but said nothing and remained with her back to Cassie.

'It's just that, well, I'd like to hire you to find someone for me.'

Harry turned towards Cassie and shook her head.

'No. No way. My career's already on thin ice and it can't take any more pressure. Not interested.'

'Please.' Cassie held her hands in front of her as if to fend off Harry's anger. 'Hear me out before you say anything. It's my husband. He's gone miss—'

'I'm not involved with the police right now,' Harry cut in. Saying the words aloud brought her a fresh wave of misery. 'I can give you a number for someone who can help. You'll bypass the switchboard, go straight to a missing persons investigator.'

Harry rummaged in her pocket hoping for a scrap of paper to scribble the number on.

'You don't understand. I can't involve the police. But I know you can help me. Please, Harry,' she begged. 'He's taken our son too and I just want my boy back. He's sick and I need to look after him. Please.' Her voice broke and her large blue eyes pleaded with Harry, who continued to shake her head.

'Maybe it would help,' she said, a touch of desperation in her voice, 'if I told you my husband's name. It's Lucas. Lucas Cavendish. Assistant Chief Constable Lucas Cavendish.'

CHAPTER THREE

The postman followed Harry down the path to her front door and shoved a small pile of post at her. She was still in a daze from her conversation with Cassie and she barely glanced at the papers in her hand. They were all circulars anyway, except for the postcard. That would be one of Charlotte's monthly missives telling her how great her life was in Silicon Valley.

Harry didn't have the stomach for reading how amazing her old friend's life was while hers was going rapidly down the pan. She threw it on top of the others in the drawer beside her front door. She'd look at it later. Right now, she needed to think.

She hadn't agreed to help Cassie but, against her better judgment, she had agreed to meet her later to find out more. Harry wasn't kidding herself. Her motives were entirely selfish. Lucas had always had it in for her and Harry thought that if she could take him down for something, she might have a good chance at getting her job back sooner. And if she didn't, at least she could make sure he was wallowing in the gutter right beside her.

—

As Harry approached Cassie's house, she was feeling unsettled. She wasn't sure she was doing the right thing talking to her. She couldn't do anything that would risk her career any further. She also couldn't sit by and wait for someone else to decide her fate. This might be her chance to take matters into her own hands. Be master of her own destiny. She'd hear what Cassie had to say, then leave. Go home and think things through. She didn't have to decide today.

Cassie's house was tucked away on the oldest and most expensive street in the town. The area was quiet and well-kept with houses of varying sizes, all added to the street at different points in history and all different in style. There were some smaller, compact dwellings and some on a much grander scale, like Cassie's. The thing they had in common, though, was space. The houses all had driveways or long, meandering paths with generous front gardens, many with brightly coloured flowers, billowing roses and green hedges to protect them from the hoi polloi wandering by. Or from each other, Harry thought as she made her way down the gravel path to Cassie's beautiful, red-brick home.

Cassie must have been waiting for her, the door opening before Harry had a chance to knock. She showed her into a large hallway, which smelt of floor polish mixed with the heady scent of rose perfume which became stronger as she leant in and, grabbing Harry by both arms, kissed her on the cheek.

Harry tensed at the intimate gesture from the stranger and stepped back quickly.

'I'm glad you came,' said Cassie. 'I wasn't sure you would.'

She led Harry along a hallway, big enough to house Harry's entire living room, to a kitchen that looked like it had been ripped from the pages of an interior magazine. There's no way any cooking happens in here – there's not a crumb or sticky patch in sight, Harry thought as she looked around.

Cassie made them both drinks, coffee from a machine that looked like it should come complete with its own barista for herself and tea from a kettle that illuminated the water into a soft blue that got darker as it boiled for Harry. They sat on tall stools at an ultra-shiny kitchen island and wherever Harry rested her hands it left smudgy fingerprints. The surface would be a SOCO's dream. She wrapped both hands tightly around her cup of tea so she couldn't mark the surface any further.

Once they were settled, Cassie began to speak.

'It's complicated.'

'Isn't it always?'

'I guess so. Let's be honest, though. Lucas being who he is makes things a lot worse.'

Cassie was playing with her necklace. A plain, gold oval locket that she was absent-mindedly rubbing between her fingers. The necklace was simple and delicate and looked mass-produced. It was at odds with the rest of Cassie's classy looking jewellery.

She had bangles on one wrist studded with colourful, sparking stones and a watch on the other that Harry knew to be expensive.

Before she was suspended, she and the team had been working on a spate of local break-ins and she'd spent a lot of time looking at the inventory of missing items, trying to track them down, waiting to see where they came up for sale. One of the watches on the list was almost identical to Cassie's and Harry knew it would cost her at least two months' salary if she wanted to own one.

'Why don't you start by telling me about Dylan?'

'He's really the reason I asked you here. He's my world. My heart and my soul. He's a proper little mummy's boy and I just want him home.' Cassie's eyes were filling with tears; she closed them, her long eyelashes almost brushing her high cheekbones.

'When Dylan was born, we thought everything was normal. And it was for a time. But I kept sensing something was wrong. He was a fussy baby. Up all night crying, and all day sometimes. I thought there might be something wrong – call it mother's instinct – but Lucas didn't agree. He thought I was overreacting. He said it was probably colic and that I just wasn't a natural mother. If I relaxed, Dylan would relax. I tried, I really did.'

Her eyes had remained closed while she was talking, but she looked solidly at Harry as she spoke the last few words as if imploring her to believe her.

Harry felt sorry for Cassie. She was clearly younger than Lucas and it sounded like he didn't reserve his superior manner for Harry. She said nothing, not wanting to interrupt the flow of the story, but she smiled encouragingly at Cassie to let her know she believed her and that she should continue.

'Anyway, one day I was at the end of my tether. Lucas was away overnight on a training course and Dylan seemed so distressed I didn't know what else to do, so I took him to the local A&E. And thank God I did. He was sick, really sick. They diagnosed him with FMF, familial Mediterranean fever. Do you know what that is?'

Harry shook her head.

'It's a genetic condition. It normally occurs when there's some Mediterranean descent in the family. My dad.' She answered the question Harry was about to ask, and as Harry looked again at Cassie, she could see that the olive tone of her skin was real, not out of a bottle like she had initially assumed.

'It causes terrible pain and inflammation if it's not treated. Breathing can become difficult. You get a swollen, painful tummy and your joints swell and become inflamed like with arthritis. Horrible.' She shuddered as she spoke. 'The condition can be managed perfectly well with regular medication, but without it....' She let the sentence hang but shook her head slowly from side to side.

Harry got the message.

'I still don't understand what's happening here, Cassie. I don't understand why Lucas has gone missing and why you won't go to the police. If he and Dylan are missing persons, they will be a priority case, even more so because of Dylan's illness. They'll start looking instantly to make sure they're safe. They can check ANPR cameras and phone round hospitals. Have you done that yet?'

'They're not in a hospital.' Cassie seemed definite about this. 'I wouldn't call Lucas a missing person either. It's not so much that he and Dylan have gone missing. It's that he's kidnapped Dylan. And he hasn't taken Dylan's medication with him. If he's not found soon, my boy will be in unbearable pain.' Her voice caught at this last comment.

At the word 'kidnapped', Harry fished her phone from her pocket and began to dial. She knew in that moment she couldn't help. This had to be dealt with properly. A team needed to be assembled quickly. Her brain was fizzing with all the things that needed to be done. Before the call could connect, Cassie had leaned across the island and knocked the phone from Harry's hand. It skidded across the slippery surface and came to rest against a large vase of colourful flowers. A tinny voice could be heard repeating

'Hello?' until Cassie swiped at the button to cut the call.

There was silence for a moment while Harry tried to digest what had just happened. The two women stared at each other from either side of the island. Nothing here was making sense.

'I'm sorry.' The words were spoken quietly by Cassie, her eyes downcast. 'Let me try and explain.'

Harry nodded for Cassie to continue but she reached for her phone, ready to call again as soon as the explanation was done, and she stood behind the stool out of arm's reach.

'Lucas is well liked by his colleagues.' She gave Harry a look that she couldn't quite interpret but that set alarm bells ringing somewhere deep inside. 'Which is why I don't think they'll look very hard for him. You see...'

Her fingers rubbed away at the locket again.

'...there's more to it than I've already said. More, that I think *you* will understand.' She looked searchingly at Harry, who was getting a very bad feeling.

'What aren't you telling me?' she asked.

'Maybe this will help to explain.' Cassie walked across the kitchen and picked up her own mobile from where it had been charging on the side. She pressed a few buttons then, finding what she was looking for, she slid the phone across the island.

Harry picked it up, not making sense of what she was seeing. She looked up at Cassie then back again at the photo Cassie had opened on the screen. The photo was of Cassie, with her hair scraped back from her face. Her face was free from makeup, but she was wearing a huge bruise that was blossoming across her left cheekbone.

The photo was full colour and Harry could make out the blues and purples of the fresh bruising that clashed with the red of Cassie's eyes where she had obviously been crying. There was also a painful-looking split on the left side of her top lip. It was swollen and a small trickle of blood had dried in the corner of her mouth.

'What is this?' Harry's mouth had gone dry. She cleared her throat and tried again. 'What am I looking at? I don't understand. What are you telling me?'

Except she did understand. She knew only too well what she was looking at.

She had spent most of her childhood looking at her mum's face and body covered with tender bruises that she painstakingly tried to cover with make-up. Although never very successfully. Sometimes there would be no covering them and they were the days Harry and Patrick would lie to the school and their friends; Mummy was at home with a migraine, she had a sickness bug, she had flu.

She wondered now how nobody had ever suspected anything – and, if they did, why hadn't someone helped? How different her life could have been if someone had stepped in. Her mum might still be alive. Harry pushed the painful thought away to concentrate on the woman in front of her.

Cassie was looking down at the photo on the phone that now lay between them, tears gathering in the corners of her eyes and spilling when they could no longer be contained.

Harry reached across and turned off the screen so that neither one of them had to look at it anymore.

'He hits me,' Cassie said, barely above a whisper. 'And I think he has taken Dylan to hurt him too.'

'I'm calling this in.' Harry pulled her phone from her pocket and again started dialling.

'No! Please!' Cassie grabbed again for the phone and, as Harry jumped back out of reach, it clattered to the floor.

'I'm sorry,' Cassie said as Harry bent to retrieve it. 'I'm sorry, but I really don't want the police involved. I know they won't believe me. He's well respected at work. Well liked. It's all a front but everyone buys it. I know you see him differently though, Harry. You don't fall for his bluster. And I know you understand.' She looked deep into Harry's eyes and rested a hand on hers. 'You get it, Harry. Please don't let my family go the same way as yours.'

The comment landed like a punch to Harry's stomach.

Maybe she could change things this time.

Maybe she could give Dylan the happy ending that she and Patrick didn't get.

'What is it you want me to do?'

'I just want you to bring Dylan home. That's all. I want my son safe and sound at home where he should be. If you can get Lucas to admit what he's done on tape, even better. If you do that, I'll take it to the police. Get him arrested. I know they won't believe it until we get proof. I'm not expecting you to do this for nothing. I'll pay you. But please decide quickly. If not, I don't know what will happen to Dylan.' At that she dissolved into tears, a low, pitiful moan echoing round the room.

Harry moved around the island to be beside Cassie and laid her arm across her shoulders. There was nothing she could say to make her feel better, but she would sit with her in solidarity for as long as she was needed.

Dan Higgins is a pilot who, for thirty years, has been flying all over the world. He lives with his wife and two sons in the city of Prague. He's a self-confessed crime fiction addict. *Czech Mate* is his first novel.

dannyhiggins@me.com

Czech Mate
The opening of a novel

'We live in an age which is so possessed by demons, that soon we shall only
be able to do goodness and justice in the deepest secrecy, as if it were a crime.'
—Franz Kafka, Prague

CHAPTER ONE

It's strange how different some things look when you actually take the time
to notice them. I was on foot, walking in the early morning sunshine. My car
was in the workshop, waiting for a part that might be available in a couple
of weeks. The mercury was already nudging northwards above twenty-five.
I'd taken off my jacket and felt small rivulets of sweat run down my back.
Walking past Prague's central library, I saw a gang of municipal labourers
working on a makeshift wooden platform above the main entrance. They
were using hammers and chisels to attack and chip away a stone frieze,
creating a shower of fine dust and small chunks of masonry. The stone
tableau was a classical design depicting Greek, or possibly Roman, figures.
I hadn't noticed the ornate carvings before. They looked like the usual
characters, toga-clad warriors wielding clubs and spears, slaying lions
and drinking wine from amphoras, offered by a couple of wanton-looking
maidens. I wondered who they'd upset to deserve such an ignoble fate; they
all seemed fairly inoffensive to me. I asked the scraggy foreman who was
smoking a roll-up why they were removing the stonework. He shrugged
and said, 'Just orders.'

It was a short time after eight when I walked through the tall, dou-
ble-doors of *Sbor národní bezpečnosti,* the National Security Corps
headquarters, next to the Ministry of the Interior on Nad Stolou. I took
the flight of stairs up to the third floor, to Directorate VI Serious Crime,
where, in a small corner, lay my office. I felt neither neat nor clean and
I definitely wished I wasn't stone-cold sober. I cursed my earlier interest
with the workmen. My shoes, trousers, shirt and hair were covered in a

fine marble dust that formed a thin, oily coating made all the worse when I tried to brush it off. I walked through the open space, where the four desks and chairs sat empty; I stepped into my office and closed the door behind.

It certainly didn't feel like a morning too different from any other. My deputy, Roman Berger, arrived at his desk about ten minutes after me. Through my closed door, I could hear his fingers tapping a two-digit tattoo on a clunky old typewriter. I sucked on the end of my pen as I put off sorting through a mound of paperwork lying on my desk, most of it procedural and pointless. The windows were open to ventilate and freshen the swampy atmosphere. Noises of the waking city, the roar of traffic, the clacks of footsteps on pavements and the blares of horns from barges on the river rose from the streets below. It was early August; the summer was hot and dry and many of the city's denizens had fled to the mountains to avoid the broiling heat. At this time of the year, crime was usually low level, mainly of the domestic variety. Sun-roasted tempers and too much alcohol always threw up enough fights, assaults and occasionally, the odd murder to keep us all gainfully employed. The Vb, the ordinary police, could deal with most of it. No, Tuesday, the second of August, 1984, wasn't too different to any other day. Nothing to show it was the day when my future would change forever. Not one simple augur to suggest that on that particular day would begin a series of events that would eventually threaten both my career and my family, along with my very life.

The bright green digits on my new electric desk clock had flicked past nine when I heard the phone ring in the main office. Berger took the call; I could hear his voice through the door, but I couldn't make out any of the conversation. After a short time, the phone on my desk rang. I picked up the receiver and heard the voice of my deputy ask me to take a phone-call. I pressed the red incoming call switch.

'Major Miler,' I said with an abruptness cultivated for the phone. 'Yes, go on.' I took a pen and scribbled down the details on an old charge sheet. 'What time was this?' I asked. 'He asked for me personally?' I stopped writing. 'Okay, okay, I'm on my way.'

I replaced the phone in its cradle, took my jacket, and opened the door into the main office. Berger glanced up with a quizzical look. He had finished his typing and had been reading the sports section of Rude Pravo about the latest news from the summer Olympics in Los Angeles.

'What is it, boss?' he asked.

I frowned. 'I'm not too sure. A report from Petrin Gardens of a body found underneath the tower. It looks like a suspicious death.'

'Doesn't really sound like a matter for you. Something for either Steffi or Curda, not a problem for a senior investigator.'

'That's the strange thing, Comrade,' I said, pulling on my jacket and checking my warrant token. 'Sergeant Zedenek asked me to attend. In person.'

'Zedenek? The Bear?' said Berger, folding his newspaper. 'He'll be drunk again. Leave it to me, Major, I'll deal with it.' He put his hands together and theatrically cracked his knuckles. 'While I'm at it, I'll give him a good kick up the arse and tell him not to bother senior investigators with such trivial matters.'

'I'd like to see you try,' I replied, smiling at the thought. 'The Sergeant's no fool. Something must have spooked him. I think if the Bear asked for me, he'll have a good reason.'

I buttoned my collar, fixed my tie and with my hand, tried to comb out most of the masonry dust still stuck in my hair. 'Come on, get a car and meet me outside. We're off for a trip to the park.'

I walked out the main door and left Berger scrabbling for his jacket, notebook and CZ-75 pistol.

CHAPTER TWO

Berger signed for an unmarked, muddy-brown Tatra while I waited outside, taking in the sunshine. Berger drove. Berger always drove: he had the gloves for it. I looked on, amused, while my deputy took time to squeeze his large hands into a pair of cream and brown leather driving gloves.

'Do they make you a better driver?' I asked.

'They don't make me any worse,' was his quick retort, as he refused to take the bait.

'You watch too many detective shows,' I said as I opened the passenger door, got into the car, and entered a furnace. The air was hot and stuffy and the plastic seats were unbearably hot.

'Yea, yea,' he replied, settling himself into the driver's seat and winding down his window. 'What about those American detective novels you collect?'

I ignored him and smiled, fastened my seatbelt, braced my feet in the footwell before grabbing the handle above the door.

'Come on, Starsky, take me to Petrin.'

Berger fired the ignition, engaged gear and drove the Tatra out of the compound in a swirl of dust, gravel and screeching rubber.

Cobbled roads, unforgiving suspension and stifling heat all came together on that uncomfortable, nerve-testing journey. Fumes, grit, and soot were the high prices to pay for the slight cooling comfort of open windows. Berger weaved the Tatra through the busy traffic, blasting the horn and using all the road, and more, on the brief ten-minute journey. He had tuned the radio to Bayern Drie, an illegal station broadcast from Munich. I was forced to listen to 'Relax', by Frank in Hollywood, or something like that. It was a banned song, deemed immoral by the Communists, but that hadn't stopped it from becoming the sound of the summer.

Petrin Gardens was one of the largest urban parks in Europe and sprawled over two hundred and eighty hectares on the left bank of the Vltava River. Its name derived from the Latin word Petrus, meaning the rocks, on account of the rocky hill that dominated the landscape. The park's main entrance was a left turn off Ujezd. A wizened old park attendant jumped to attention and raised the hurdle before pointing us through the gates towards a narrow avenue of neatly trimmed trees and well-tended borders. Berger navigated us along this small access road, nothing more than a narrow path used for gardeners, that wound around the steep rocky hill on the western side of the park. The track rose sharply and the massive oaks and walnut trees soon gave way to smaller cherry, beech and limes. Views of manicured parkland, orchards and rose-covered terraces were visible through the gaps in the thick foliage that lined our way. The road bisected the metal tracks of the funicular that carried the less energetic visitors to the top of the hill. Berger slowed the vehicle as the path steepened, becoming broken and uneven. Our ride was becoming something similar to a roller coaster at a summer fair, and I swore when my head banged off the roof after we crashed through a bomb-sized crater on the path.

'Sorry about that, boss,' said Berger, a grin plastered on his face.

'You look it,' I replied, wincing as we struck another rut in the dusty dry clay track. A light-coloured crenelated wall ran along the left side of the path and up ahead, on top of the crest of the hill. I could make out a small church building. One last turn and we were out of the trees, on to level ground and drove into a narrow, paved area outside the Church of St Lawrence.

The Baroque chapel, with its green copper towers and orange washed walls, looked incongruous against the parkland setting. I remember reading that it was originally a medieval pilgrim site, where ancient penitents crawled on their knees to pray for health and forgiveness. The current building dated from the 1750s, but was no longer used for religious ceremonies, not since the Communist Party's crackdown on religion. The Party always had a problem with the church; often imprisoning, deporting, or disappearing many of its priests and bishops. Religion represented something of an anathema to the communists, something beyond their control and influence; their only solution was proscription and persecution. I noticed the steps of the chapel's entrance carpeted with a sea of candles, crucifix and icons. It was easy to believe each one represented both a religious belief and also a minor act of defiance.

We drove towards two yellow and white Vb patrol cars parked at the far end of the courtyard. Berger killed the engine, and we both unpeeled ourselves from the hot, sticky vinyl seats. I wiped the sweat from my forehead, flattened my wavy blond hair and once again tried to rub off some of the marble dust from my trousers. In front of us, looming out of the tall trees and dominating the surrounding landscape, was the Petrin Tower; its cold, grey metal structure framed in a sun-bleached, powder-blue sky.

CHAPTER THREE

Berger and I silently walked towards a group of khaki-clad police standing around a covered object near the base of the tower. One of them broke away from the others and walked to meet us. He was a mountain of a man, over two metres tall, with barrel-thick legs and huge hairy arms that hung from wide powerful shoulders. It looked like somewhere there must be a bridge missing its troll. Dressed in the uniform of a Senior Sergeant of the *Veřejná bezpečnost,* he wore triple stars above the three stripes on his rolled-up sleeves. As he approached, I could almost feel his presence; the man appeared to possess his own gravitational pull. His uniform was stretched and strained to near breaking point, and his beer- and sausage-fed belly hung low over his shiny black service belt.

'Good morning, Jarra,' I said to the man who I knew all too well: Sergeant Jaroslav Zedenek, or the Bear as he was called by his comrades, but only behind his back.

'Major,' he replied, nodding to me. 'Lieutenant,' he added to Berger, in a deep baritone voice that boomed from a mouth lost in a thick, black bushy beard.

'Comrade Zedenek, what have you got for us that's so important?' asked Berger, with more than a little annoyance in his tone.

'Unnatural death,' said the sergeant, addressing me while rubbing his beard with a hairy paw. 'Male, middle-aged. By the looks of it, he's suffered multiple head and neck injuries.'

He turned away and walked towards the green tarpaulin.

'Have you found any identification on the body?' I asked.

'No, we haven't touched anything yet. We waited for you to arrive.'

'Why not?' asked Berger. His surprise sounded as genuine as mine.

'You'll see, Lieutenant,' said the giant without turning around. 'You'll see.'

Zedenek was an experienced man with over thirty years of service in the Vb, the ordinary police. He had dealt with most difficulties the city could throw at him. I thought his behaviour was a little bit more than odd. He was usually far from shy, never slow to take the initiative when needed. The Bear believed in an old-fashioned approach, and he was often involved in various disciplinary hearings when his own brand of intuitive policing resulted in complaints from the public.

Berger passed me a pair of latex gloves he'd retrieved from his pocket; I pulled them on, hoping they were not from the batch that gave me a rash.

He did the same and asked, 'Would you mind if I got away from the office early this evening? I've got hockey practice and...'

'Sure, fine by me,' I replied while taking in the surrounding scene.

As we followed in the Sergeant's wake, I saw two men to my left, homeless Roma Gypsies by the look of them, sitting on a park bench near the entrance to the funicular. Two Vb privates were talking to them, but they were all too far away for me to overhear the conversation. They looked rough and one of them, the smaller of the two, appeared to be agitated and arguing with the uniformed officers. We approached the other group of police who were standing and smoking around an olive-green canvas tarpaulin, a standard issue for all Vb patrols. From underneath I saw a foot sticking out, like from underneath a bed sheet. The trouser had ridden up, revealing sad mottled-blue flesh above a black sock and shoe. I noticed a couple of privates quickly stamp out their cigarettes and move away as we neared.

'This is a crime scene, comrades,' I shouted towards the retreating men. 'Have you not read the new directives on protecting evidence?' I added, thinking the modern techniques of criminal detection were slow to permeate down to the rank-and-file uniformed officers.

Stopping beside the green tarp, the Bear's thick leather belt creaked and groaned as he bent down and pulled back the cover. I'd seen plenty of dead bodies during my time on the Directive; none of them were pretty. This one was no different. It was a mess of legs and arms bent at impossible angles, coming together to form a crumpled, contorted tangle of death. The body was male. He was lying face down, and I guessed his age to be in his late thirties or early forties. His neck looked broken and I could see deep bruising above a white shirt collar. A pool of blood had spread and dried in a sticky puddle from under the left side of the corpse, exciting the attention of the early morning flies.

Apart from the obvious damage, the man appeared reasonably fit and healthy, certainly not one of the homeless who inhabited the park during the warm summer months. His dark navy suit looked stylishly expensive and the brown leather brogues appeared handmade. I guessed he was wearing more than I earned in a year.

'Nice suit,' said Berger wistfully. 'And I'll bet those shoes are foreign.'

I glanced towards the Sergeant, who didn't hold my gaze but looked away. Now I understood his reticence. The death of a foreigner was a whole high-rise above his pay grade. I couldn't blame him and quickly said a brief secret prayer to St Michael the Archangel that the body belonged to a fellow Czechoslovak. The death of a foreign national meant dealing directly with our Ministry of Foreign Affairs, their endless forms and difficult technocrats. Worse still, I could almost hear the heavy jackboots of the Secret Police inevitably trampling all over the case; the thought of the StB, their clumsy, ruthless methods and departmental overreach simply filled me with dread. No, I could easily forgive the Sergeant, this one time.

Berger and I stood on either side of the body and both eased down on our haunches for a closer look. The potent smell of death and alcohol rising from the corpse was both eye-watering and gut-wrenching. A squadron of flies bombed and harried the body. I slapped away a couple who decided to take a break on my face. I felt sweat trickle down my back. With no spoken command, we each took hold of the left shoulder, and with a great deal of effort, slowly rolled the body over on to its back.

'Shit,' I said.

Zedenek whistled while Berger simply groaned.

There, lying before us, was the bloodied, alabaster face of one of the most recognisable and important citizens in all of Czechoslovakia. Never again would he open a factory, kiss a reluctant toddler, or give a rousing speech at a Party Congress. For there, lying on his broken back, with dry lifeless eyes, like three-day-old fish on a counter, staring into bleak infinity, was the body of David Beran, Minister of Finance and the rising star of the Communist Party.

'Hey Berger,' I said, without looking away from the body. 'I don't fancy your chances of getting away early tonight.'

Berger groaned once more.

CHAPTER FOUR

Amid a few disgruntled comments from the uniformed officers, I tasked Zedenek and his men with securing the scene. Three officers marked off an area of about one-hundred-metres around the body with bright yellow tape. I saw The Bear and one of his section unceremoniously move the two homeless men from the park bench situated just inside the secured area.

Berger returned to the car and radioed the details back to headquarters, kick-starting the slow, lumbering machinations of bureaucratic investigation. Alone, I took a closer examination of the corpse and the surrounding area. I had little time before the forensic directorate arrived, with all their tools and cameras; now was my last chance to take a careful look at the relatively undisturbed scene.

I could taste bitter morning coffee in my mouth as I knelt down beside the body. I paused for a moment. The air was still and quiet, broken only by birdsong from nearby trees and the faint hum of city traffic. Under a shimmering, sun-fuelled haze, the city's famous spires and towers appeared unfocused, indistinct, as if in another shadow world. I took a deep breath and experienced a sense of detachment from the present, an otherness, one million miles away from the hustle of the city and the offensive obscenity lying at my feet. It was a fleeting sensation that didn't last long; the buzzing, dive-bombing flies kicked me out of my reverie, back to the here and now, and grim reality.

Disturbing as little as possible, I scoured the immediate area around the body, but couldn't discern anything unusual. A small leather satchel hung over the right shoulder of Beran. I pulled it out from under his corpse. Unfastening a simple clasp, I carefully prised the bag open. Inside were some brown cardboard files, embossed with the Czechoslovak Ministry of Finance motif. I used a pen to ease the top file open and pulled out a sheet of paper with the tips of my fingers. It was a simple page containing a list of names, numbers, and addresses. The other files contained similar sheaves of pages. At the bottom of the satchel was Beran's KSC, *Komunistická strana Československa,* membership book. The picture on the inside cover was of a much younger man, in his prime, leaner, with a clear complexion, without the worry-lines and broken veins of age. I knew the minister was forty-three, only six years older than myself, but I hadn't seen him in the flesh for over a decade. It didn't seem so long since he'd first appeared on the political scene when he walked with a swagger and possessed a confidence that radiated to all who met and heard him. We used to say he possessed, what they called in the West, star quality. Also in the bag was his gaudy, snake-skin wallet. Inside I found three thousand Koruna, five hundred US Dollars along with a collection of bills, tickets and receipts. It was certainly a tidy sum, more than many could earn in five years. Looking at the receipts, I realised the minister had expensive tastes. I made a cursory search of the body, checking the pockets, belt, and shoes. Berger was correct – they were Italian, and the suit was from London. In Beran's left trouser pocket, I discovered a small key on a plain metal fob. It looked too small for a house key; I guessed it looked more like something to lock a drawer or cupboard. Almost unconsciously, I placed it in my jacket inside pocket and continued my search.

I looked up at the tower that scaled up before me. Beran's injuries were consistent with a fall. It was all too easy to assume the body had fallen from above. But I never liked to assume anything. I wanted to be sure.

I heard footsteps behind me.

'Well?' I asked.

'The Colonel wants you back at headquarters immediately,' was Berger's reply.

'Of course he does,' I said.

'He was very insistent.'

'I've no doubt about that.'

I turned towards my deputy; his face was silhouetted against the blinding light.

'He's worried. He thinks a difficulty like this could be dangerous for him.' I looked around, making sure there was no one within earshot. 'Dangerous for all of us.'

'Why is that?' asked Berger.

'No matter how this senior Party official ended up here, this unfortunate business will look bad for the KSC. The bosses will demand it's handled with a delicate touch; tidied up, put to rest and buried in a lead-lined casket. Gone, forgotten, brushed out of public consciousness, all within a week, no doubt.'

I looked down at Beran's shattered remains.

'The Colonel will lecture me, provide just enough rope, and if there are any mistakes, be there to hang me from the tallest tree.'

'Colonel Smit would never do a thing like that. He's one of us,' said Berger, shaking his head.

I laughed.

'He's one of us alright, but he's also a senior officer. Better than most, granted. But remember – he's only climbed to the top of the slippery pole by ensuring there are enough of us below to break his fall if he should ever lose his grip.'

I took out a handkerchief from my jacket pocket and wiped a trickle of sweat running down the back of my neck.

'It's the way of the world everywhere, Berger. You know that.'

I stood up, my knees cracking in protest.

'Come on, I want to get a look at the top of that tower,' I said, walking towards the entrance.

'The Colonel said he wanted to see you immediately,' reminded Berger.

'We better hurry then, Comrade.'

CHAPTER FIVE

Petrin Tower stood some sixty-four metres above the hill it was built upon and gave visitors a commanding view of the city laid out below to the east. Originally built as a temporary construction, its popularity with the public ensured it was now one of the most popular tourist sites in the city. The structure was similar to Eiffel's more famous Parisian creation. Five main stanchions supported a central octagonal tube that housed an elevator, which provided access to the two lookout platforms. Assembled in a series of lattice-worked grey steel, two double staircases wrapped themselves around a central lift-shaft in a double helix, one for ascending and the other descending. At the base was a white-washed stone building with a grey lead roof that acted as a ticket and information office. Walking towards the entrance, I remembered the long queues of summer crowds waiting in line, often overwhelming the elderly ticket orderlies who charged a ten-Koruna entrance fee. Visitors came from all the Comecon nations, lured by the view and tempted with tacky replica models sold from the gift shops and stalls pitched around the base of the tower. During the summer months, it was not unusual to hear western accents, often students on exchange programmes, among the crowds that queued for entrance. I avoided the tower during the tourist season, preferring to take my wife Anna and son Jakub in the spring and autumn when visitors were sparse and the city looked its best.

A nervous-looking man stood by the entrance door. He was wearing faded blue overalls, worn work boots and a flat, checked cap. He was of medium height, thin and aged; his dark complexion was common to those who laboured in the outdoors. He looked nervous as a kitten and removed his cap as I approached.

'You are?' I asked.

'Kehllner, sir. Chief gardener,' he replied, looking down at his boots.

'So, Comrade, was it you who found the body?'

'Yes, sir. Me and the rest of my cadre.'

'Go on then, tell me what you found,' I said.

'We arrived around seven-thirty, as usual, and started with our daily tasks.'

'Which are?' asked Berger.

'We load the vans with our tools and set off to ready the park for opening at nine. We empty the rubbish bins, sweep the public paths, wash down the entrance halls and the viewing platforms.'

He squeezed his cap like a farmer wringing a chicken's neck.

'We also have to chase away the tramps who use the park as a dossing ground. Later in the day, we attend to our scheduled maintenance jobs. When we arrived at the Tower this morning, we immediately saw the body. It was just lying there.' His voice tailed off as he replayed the scene in his mind.

'Did you touch it?' I asked.

'No,' he replied. 'I sent a comrade to raise the alarm.'

'Did you notice anything else unusual?'

'No, nothing I can think of. Nothing out of the ordinary...' He paused and took a deep gulp. '...apart from the dead body.'

I looked behind him, at the basic lock on the tower's heavy wooden entrance door. Hanging from the keyhole was a bunch of rusty keys on a crude metal ring.

'Is this door locked at night?' I asked the gardener.

'Yes,' he replied. 'It's locked by the ticket attendants when the tower closes at eight. They leave the keys at the porter's office by the gate. We collect the keys in the morning so we can clean the tower before opening to the public at nine.'

'Who unlocked the door this morning?' asked Berger.

'I did,' said the gardener. 'After we found the body, I thought we might continue with our tasks while we waited for the police to arrive. It was only after I opened it the thought struck me you might not want us going inside.'

'Good man,' I said. 'You have more sense than most of my officers.'

He blew out his cheeks with relief and appeared more relaxed. I detected sharp intelligence behind his cloudy blue eyes. 'So, no one has been inside this morning?'

'No, sir, I made sure all the men stayed away until we had permission.'

'And you are sure the door was locked when you arrived?' I asked.

'Yes, I'm positive.'

'Is there any other entrance to the tower, apart from this one?'

'No, this is the only way in,' he replied.

I glanced at Berger, who simply raised his eyebrows.

'Well, thank you, Comrade, for all your help. That will be all for now, but we may need to speak to you again.'

'Thank you, sir.' The gardener hesitated and again looked down at his boots. 'Sorry Major, but what time do you think we can get inside to clean up for opening? The park commissar will breathe down my neck to get things moving as soon as possible.'

'Not today, Comrade,' I said. 'I'm afraid Petrin will not reopen until we've finished our investigations. Don't worry Kehllner, I'll deal with the Commissar if you have any problems.'

I walked through the entrance into a small area that faced a staircase on one side and an elevator's double-door on the other. Berger moaned at the large red *Mimo Provoz* sign hanging from a piece of tape stuck onto the lift's steel doors. I was secretly glad it was out of service; I long suffered from a phobia of elevators and always preferred stairs if offered the choice. We split up and scanned around the room that encircled the central lift shaft, searching for anything that might be relevant. We met each other again by the entrance without either of us finding anything unusual.

I turned to Berger and said, 'If the body fell from above, then Beran must have used the stairs to get up there.'

'I agree,' he replied, looking up the staircase. 'That's the only way.'

Mark King has won numerous short-fiction competitions and appeared in multiple anthologies. He previously studied creative writing at York and Cambridge and is the founder of the influential #vss365 writing community that provides inspiration for new writers and bestselling authors, reaching millions of impressions daily.

@making_fiction
www.makingfiction.com
markaking@outlook.com

Oxbridge: Creation
The opening of a crime novel

DAY ONE: LIGHT
Chapter One: Brona

Death is a switch. A state of being. Life equals on. Death equals off.

Brona is the operator of a switch which makes the world better. She removes human leeches and parasites. It is more than a job; she thinks of it as a calling. A responsibility.

She lets Oxbridge City seep into her pores. There, beyond the tourist merch and ornate towers, is the pungent stench of entitlement, of power, of the elite passing the baton down, generation after generation. Like the pounding of an industrial factory, it reverberates around the country, the continent, the globe – she's felt its presence from the moment she was born. Perhaps before.

The city is unceasing and remorseless. It hammers, batters, pummels, and strikes. History may change, but Oxbridge seldom does. Despite the polarised sides of the city, Oxford on the west, Cambridge on the east, the combined city is a cookie-cutter machine sustaining the world-order of things for almost a millennium. The machine created by the elite to keep their position unassailable never sleeps, and it never runs out of benefactors to fuel it.

Brona's task today is not simple. It requires guile to make it look natural, at least long enough to leave the scene. Guns are a last resort. They are devoid of creativity; they lack... finesse. Her job today is a task, an item on a list, an inventory to complete. Brona takes no pleasure in pain and death. It is simply necessary, in the same way an oncology surgeon cuts patients to remove cancer.

In order for evil to thrive, it only takes that good women do nothing.

While working, she likes to harness the power of visualisation. Using every sense to make a future possibility real, so solid it becomes inevitable.

She draws on the world around her.

She strides to meet the tour group. They wait below on the neutral islands, *the Void* as some call it, that separate Oxford from Cambridge. She glances down at the gathering group as she crosses the bridge where the Cam and the Cherwell rivers merge. She runs her hand over the rough stonework of the bridge wall, which is eroded by history and battered by pollution. Cambridge is behind her. The long-dead eyes of the scientists, polymaths, and rebellious titans who have walked those streets almost tug at Brona's overcoat. And in front, Oxford, with its intimidating statues of political giants, even today the shadow of its buildings wraps round future world leaders like a cloak.

Between these two opposing worlds, Brona's fingers sink into a patch of spongy moss on the lip of the bridge wall, and she recalls a sense of something. Yes, she can feel it now – the popping eyeballs of a previous target as she pressed her fingers into the mush, quarrying deeper until she could tunnel no more.

The bridge is twenty, maybe thirty, feet above the river. As her hand continues to run over the brittle stone, a fist-size piece dislodges and drops riverside. She holds her breath. She doesn't want to draw undue attention to herself. Nothing to see here. She marches on. Elongated silence greets her until she hears the splash. It's not like hearing the liquid thud of a body being dropped from a height – but it's close enough.

A phone-zombie smashes into her. The fella wears a cheap suit and a cocky sneer. He staggers back. His mouth agape, he registers surprise that he's barely knocked Brona. 'Sorry, sugar,' he says.

Sugar? Is he from another decade? Brona gives him a half-smile. Enough to be polite, not enough to encourage him. 'No problem,' she says. She wants to say more. Like if he wasn't so distracted by his phone addiction, he would have noticed her, seen people, had comprehension of the world as he struts through it. But she says nothing. She glances at his suit, vintage middle-of-German-supermarket aisle; she can almost feel the static electricity pulling her hair towards the fabric. She remembers another occasion. Different fella, better suit, that one cried, then he soiled himself. But he was planned; it was legitimate.

'Let me make it up to you, babe,' Mr Polyester says. His breath is sour coffee with a tinge of synthetic sweetness. He licks his lips. She considers the taste. She's tasted something similar before, the sickly taste of death from the lips of the last man who tried to manipulate her. Brona's toes are curled inside her boots, like they're pinning her to the bridge, rooting her to the city, and the job – *don't engage, no matter how tempting it is. Stick to the target.* She can't afford to be remembered. She smiles again and strides forward.

'Whatevs,' he shouts to her back. A bloke like him won't remember her. 'Your loss, I wouldn't have swiped you if I'd seen you on the app anyhows.'

Brona ignores his baiting and paces forward. The tour group is bigger now. Almost full size. Big enough to join unnoticed.

The smell from the river is musty. Like it's full of bathwater tipped from the buildings of the infant medieval city. Nothing like the smell of a burning body that one time – pork crackling – it lingered in her nostrils long after she fled the scene. Will the new target smell like this once the job is done?

Brona reflects on the visualisation she has performed as she paces across the bridge.

Her hands are taut. She squeezes them. Releases them.

In another job she might be called a futurist or a prophet. The switch operator knows what the world is today and what it will be tomorrow. She knows what will happen if she doesn't act. The pulverising migraines that needle and stab behind her eyes have been less severe, less frequent, since she accepted her calling.

Thinking ahead, visualising what is to come, she knows, like the first day of creation in the Bible, there will be light. She imagines her target lit up like an angel. The smell, the sounds. Another job completed. There will be life. Then there won't. One person fewer who has poisoned the world rather than contributed to it.

The scene is set, and now the play needs to draw to its inevitable conclusion. The target stands in front of Brona. Without the glow of electricity around her she's no angel to look at, granted, but she's who Brona's here to kill. The first target of a new job always has the greatest pressure. But Brona is ready. Being prepared is a philosophy for scouts – and contract killers.

Brona watches her target breathe. She breathes so leisurely and instinctively, like the shadow of death has not come for her today.

She goes about her business, blissfully unaware as Brona surveys her from the back of the crowd. Brona is just a shadow, one of many; nobody here will remember her. The target's chunky body barely moves as she scoops in the frosty morning air.

Brona thinks of Nina Simone. The music fills her soul. It is a new start – a new contract.

Brona closes her eyes for the briefest moment. The inane babble of the tourist group dampens as she narrows her focus. The pull of gravity weighs her body to the ground and she imagines she is the axis on which the world rotates.

Eyes open. Breathe deeply. Observe. Assess. Learn. Brona matches the breathing pattern of the target. In her slow, rhythmic heartbeat, Brona connects to the city and is ready to fulfil her purpose.

She knows to be here, on the islands that separate Oxford to the west and Cambridge to the east, is risky. It's not wise to be so near a target in a public place. Her professional instincts have always told her to avoid it, but this kill needs to be visible and spectacular. Brona has her list. She has her remit.

The islands are like the small, uneasy gap between conjoined twins. The river cut in two. The city spliced. Each side has a personality, independent thought, and instincts. Each side has a soul. But like the twins, the two sides of the city are fused and they can't escape each other. They are forever bound in this time and place, separated by two rivers on either side of a tiny outcrop of islands.

Brona observes her target, the tour guide.

The target is oblivious. Brona is almost invisible. Brona feels like a cormorant eyeing a fish that is too wrapped up in its world to comprehend that there is even a sky above.

Her target swims contentedly, smugly, safely protected in her world.

The target's name badge says Rosemary Harrington-Page. Brona doesn't need to know she's never been called Rose, Mary, or heaven forbid, Rosie.

Rosie wears her Oxford Blue, dark blue, imperial blue, don't-fuck-with-the-rules blue. Blue the colour of authority, of police, of the ties and scarves that adorn the bespoke wardrobes of world leaders and petrochemical CEOs. She talks with a plummy air of power and when she laughs with her fake theatrical chortle, her body jiggles against her strained uniform. Brona's client assured her that Rosie is a legitimate target.

'Ladies, gentlemen, dear beloved friends of Oxford University,' Rosie says. 'If you look to your left, the west of the islands, you can see the beauty of the *original* university city, Oxford, before students corrupted and exploited it, before forming Cambridge University on the other side of the river.'

When she says Cambridge, her lips curl, and there is a crinkle in her forehead like scrunched wastepaper. The last time Brona saw that look was on a child who had Coke fizz in their nasal canal.

Rosie corrals her group towards her as she weaves backwards and forwards, building up the tension. The crowd is a kaleidoscope of nationalities. The only thing unifying them is the Oxford-branded scarves, hats and supposedly classy merch. Brona's fellow tourists say nothing but they silently shout that they all belong to the same tribe.

'Walk with me!' Rosie demands. They all follow, transfixed.

Brona joins the moving wave of Oxford-Blue plankton. She, too, is wearing the same tribal tourist tat. Always best to fit in.

They pass by a tree, bent and gnarled with age. Rosie throws her hands in the air. 'This is the famous Hanging Tree. Possibly one of the most important sites in the whole of Oxbridge City. Can anyone tell me why?' Rosie glares at her group expectantly. It's as if the group are letting her down. 'I said, can *anyone* tell me why?' she shouts a little louder. She has the air of a deranged kids-entertainment leader at a caravan park.

An American accent braves the tundra of silence. 'Yes, *ma'am*,' he says. 'Is this where they hanged the Oxford townspeople for framing the innocent students?'

Brona watches Rosie closely and counts down from ten as she can see Rosie turn from coral pink to afterburner red, and through to explosive plumb. 'Innocent?' Rosie bellows.

The American man shrinks back a little, but he bravely or foolishly continues. 'Yes, *ma'am*. Back in 1208, the townspeople didn't like the students who were all clerics, religious men. The people of Oxford planned to kill an innocent woman and then blame the students.'

'Oh, it seems we have a history expert in our midst,' Rosie mocks. If her Oxford employment and allegiance were not already clear, then she leaves them all in no doubt. 'Are you sure your colours are right, sir? Shouldn't you be wearing Cambridge Blue, or pond-slime green, as I like to call it?'

Brona knows the tourists lap up the rivalry. The city is built on division, it forces people to choose allegiances, culture, philosophy. Choosing Oxford or Cambridge taps into people's core values and beliefs. Maybe Rosie is playing along. Brona's seen other tourist guides do it, but Rosie is in a league of her own.

'I'm Oxford through and through,' the American man protests.

If Brona stood between them, Rosie's glare might cut her in half.

'Sure you are, sir. You're one of our own, of that there is no doubt. Do tell us more, Mr Oxford.' The tour guide dares him.

Brona's fellow tour group falls silent. Brona can almost hear the cogs in the guy's brain. His wife pushes him. 'Go on, Art, she's no better than you. You tell everyone the story. It's in the history books, after all.'

'Yes, Art, do tell me – tell everyone,' Rosie goads, her hands cupped over her ears. 'Well, *Art*, I'm waiting!'

Art seems to get a second wind with his wife behind him. 'The king was using Oxford. He was on bad terms with Rome. The students were caught in the middle. The townspeople wanted the students out. They had tried a few times, but the king protected them. However, the townspeople figured that not even the king could protect the students if they had committed a murder. Then mob justice would take over.'

Brona can't work out if Rosie is going to explode with rage or laughter.

'They set the students up,' Art continues. 'A woman was about to be murdered and the students were to be blamed. But they caught the plotters red-handed. The townsfolk had to rely on the king to intervene and settle the peace. He sent envoys, and they promised the students whatever they wanted. They asked for land on the other side of the city to set up a new place of learning, somewhere that would welcome freedom of thought, science and innovation.'

'Well, you do have a vivid imagination, Art,' Rosie taunts. 'Perhaps you should stand up here and run the tour? I reckon I should pay to listen to you.'

There are a few nervous laughs from the crowd. Rosie is not to be messed with. Even Art and his wife go quiet.

'That's what the historians from the Cambridge side wanted you to believe,' Rosie says. Her colour has returned and she's regained control. 'The other version of events is that the students actually killed someone. The townspeople apprehended and hanged a handful of students on that same tree. They chased the remaining rebels out of the city. The students intended to create a new place of learning, where Little Cambridge is today in the swamp-laden fens in the east. Still, the good people of Oxford forgave them, welcomed them back and, in the genuine spirit of Christianity, allowed them to build on the other side of the river.'

Brona glances around. Nobody's buying it.

Rosie ushers the group towards the stone stairwell to the east of *the Void*. The narrow, curved footbridge connects this small island to the Cambridge side, just north of where Magdalen Bridge becomes King's College Bridge. It is one of the few places that allows pedestrians to cross to *the Void*. They leave the Cherwell River behind and head towards The Backs, crossing over the Cam and looking towards the Cam-side majestic view of King's College Chapel. Beneath them, Cambridge-Blue livery adorns the punts, and Cam-blue hats and scarves garnish the puntsmen. They're hollering for business like it's an East End market stall.

'We punt from the back, not the front. Cambridge puts people first, not like Oxford. Come ride the Cam, not the Cherwell,' one of the gosling-young punters hollers.

'You are mistaken,' Rosie says. 'We're not interested in anything you offer. We're crossing the river, just once, just today.'

'Ah, the environmentalist protests, Ox-side?' the puntsman shouts.

'Yes,' Rosie replies, marching them towards Cam-side. 'We have special permission for me to host the tour on your side today.'

'Forgive my French, *ma'am*, but the bloody protestors are here as well,' he shouts.

'But there are fewer of them and at least they haven't closed your buildings down,' Rosie replies. 'We don't need your wonky punt, young man. We have special permission to visit the hidden tunnels that run next to the Cam.'

The gosling looks forlornly at his punt before leaving to hustle more tourists.

Brona and the other tourists nudge themselves over the thin, collapsed-vein bridge and disembark on Cam-side where the lush, freshly mown green spaces behind King's College Chapel and Gibbs' welcome them to Cambridge. This is *the Backs*, the beautiful Backs. It is a stark contrast to the Ox-side greeting this tour would typically have. Magdalen Tower would have greeted them like a sentry guarding the west from the east. Brona knows that back in the day it would have been a foreboding sign to the rebels, scientists, and heretics who dared to approach from Cam-side. Brona has taken advantage of the timing and the changed route; fewer buildings mean much less CCTV on this side.

As per Rosie's observation, the protests Cam-side are fewer, more dispersed and less organised than Ox-side. Many of the protestors look like students. They are passionately gesticulating, shouting, chanting, flourishing placards and banners in meaningless patterns like they're on a bad acid trip. Many have slogans on the same theme:

If God created the world in seven days
We have seven days to save it

They pause as Rosie tries to figure a way of navigating the group safely away from what looks like a posh riot club.

'Excuse me, Rosemary,' Art pipes up. 'What's this all about?'

Rosie ignores him as she cuts a path through the rabble.

Brona watches as one of the tour group, a towering man with a Germanic accent, responds to Art. 'Didn't you see any of this on the news?' Art shrugs, which the German man takes as his opportunity to continue.

'An environmentalist extremist group has been pressurising Oxford and Cambridge to divest their funding of fossil fuels. It's a big deal. You know Jamie Greenacre, right?'

Brona steps back. The students and grimy protestors with their matted hair and moth-eaten jumpers are shouting, screaming – their spittle is in the air; their banners and placards are nursery-style competent, with rhymes that match. They thrust their messages, verbal and physical, at anyone who doesn't seem to match their ferocity or veracity. Brona watches Rosie. The tour guide slows, her ear tilted towards her two sheep, lost and distracted in the flock of scattered protesting wolves. Brona can barely hear them in the crowd, but Rosie has the air of a teacher who can notice a whisper in a classroom of chaos.

One protester stops; they can't be over twenty. The protestor faces Art. 'Be careful what you say. You are tourists just passing through,' they insist.

'Who the hell are you, lady?' Art responds.

'Lady? How dare you assume my gender!'

Art is standing open-mouthed. Brona figures he's unsure how to dig himself out of the situation without the threat of being *cancelled* in public.

'*We* are Annihilation Resistance!' the person screams in his face. 'We're here because we have no choice. Jamie Greenacre has tried everything he can. Oxford won't listen, nor will Cambridge. We're not just here to protect the city you've come to visit. No, this is far bigger than just a city. This is *the* last stand. A new start before the end comes for all of us.'

Art's confusion is written in his eyes. 'Why is it such a big deal?' he asks the protester. 'Surely, it's *just* two universities? Why don't you target the government, the big corporations?'

The student becomes twitchy – it's as if someone has somehow charged their multiple piercings with mild electricity. 'What happens in Oxford and Cambridge makes a difference. They educate future world leaders over there,' the student says as they aggressively point back towards Ox-side. 'Companies invest billions in research. Technology thrives. Science is king this side,' they say, pointing a finger to the ground the group stands on. 'All things that can change the world, yet Oxford and Cambridge continue to invest in fossil fuels. Their lack of ethics is ingrained in the very fabric of our culture. It stains every decision made globally. Jamie Greenacre has served notice. We can't create a new world, but we have seven days to save the one we have.'

Oxford-Blue Rosie grimaces and almost growls at the student. She leans back and tugs Art towards her. Rosie rolls her eyebrows like she's seen it all before.

'Follow me, ladies and gentlemen,' she hollers across the crowd. 'The tour must go on.'

The group shoals towards a small gate and metal railings which are in front of the Kennedy Buildings. Rosie flashes her Ox-Blue badge at the burly security guard who protects the barrier like it's Downing Street.

'That won't get you in here, miss,' he says.

'Miss?' Rosie snarls.

'Sorry,' he replies. 'That will not get you in here, madam.'

'We have permission,' Rosie snaps. 'I couldn't take them to the tunnels on my side so I had to come over here. It's not like it's my choice, but there is a reciprocal arrangement if the same thing happens to any of your tour guides.'

He bites his lip. 'How many in your group?' he says, puffing his chest out and tensing his biceps as he crosses his arms.

'Thirteen, including me,' Rosie replies.

His eyes narrow. 'You know we really shouldn't be letting anyone in today, given the... situation,' he says.

'But I'm not just anyone, am I?' Rosie says, looking at his ID card. 'I am a member of staff with agreed permission and the right to be here today. Are you refusing to let me in? This is scheduled regardless of the demonstrations, Dan-nee,' Rosie sneers, elongating his name like an unpleasant taste on her tongue. Brona notices a small smile on Rosie's face, like she's enjoying the conflict. 'Now, I know it's hard for you to cope with dozens of protestors, but the roads and buildings are closed my side. Try being a security guard over there.'

A voice somewhere in the dark, beyond the locked gates, shouts, 'Let them in, Danny. She's authorised.'

Danny gives Rosie a fake smile and opens the gate, which sounds like it's not been oiled this century.

They clamber through. Danny clicks them in with a hand-held counter. Brona knows the count will be two short on the way out.

Danny points the group to a box where phones need to be stored. Where the group is going, photography is strictly forbidden. There are inevitable grumbles, but the choice is simple. Keep your phone and you miss out on the most exclusive element of the tour.

On previous reconnaissance, Brona checked out the CCTV. Outside, agitated crowds will obscure the view and the operators will focus on the apparent risk they pose. Inside, the CCTV might as well be non-existent.

They're reliant on physical security and guards. It's the armadillo approach – hard and crunchy on the outside, soft in the middle.

They huddle through a narrow archway and descend into the sickly glow of tungsten bulbs struggling against the ancient darkness of the man-made tunnels. Motion sensors control the lights – a pathetic sticking plaster to show how *green* they are. This is no typical church crypt or even where they keep their famous collections of vintage wines. No, this is a secret maze of dark channels, roughly hacked alcoves, uneven nooks and sacred catacombs that were only opened to tourists last year.

Rosie, the queen of melodrama, gesticulates as she enlightens her tour group. 'There are signs of secret, possibly *satanic*, Templar ceremonies down here, but more on that later.' The path ahead is narrow, single-line only. Beyond is a chamber where Rosie will enact a fake Templar ceremony with the sort of gusto that might interest the world-famous Footlights drama group. She continues to ensure the tour group has no doubts about her extensive knowledge – Brona has seen no one as desperate for a five-star Trip Advisor rating. And given she is with friends, Oxford fanatics on her tour, her OTT performances might just get it. 'They also used these tunnels as Second World War vaults for precious collections and bunkers for senior academics to seek shelter.'

Not long now.

The tunnel leading to the chamber is snug around the group and the tall German man struggles to fit through. Rosie's at the front, Art and his wife behind her, the rest of the group follow, and Brona's at the rear, where she needs to be.

They pass two mains-powered caged inspection lamps – emergency lighting. The motion sensor triggers the next set of lights. The signal.

Now.

Now it's time.

Above, Brona hears the overhead lights buzz, witnesses them flicker, yet they are stubbornly refusing to go off. She worries, momentarily, that she has not tampered with the lighting power supply enough.

Then, gloriously, the lights fail.

At first, people are scrambling for the phones they don't have. Rosie shouts out. 'Be calm. Everything is fine. Whoever is at the back, please find one of the inspection torches and pass it up to me. There are emergency sockets all along the route. Like most electrical systems, the mains and lighting are on different circuits. I'll need to plug it in up here. This happens sometimes. Don't panic. Just pass one along and everything will be fine.'

The mature lady beside Brona reaches for the first torch before Brona hands her the second one with her gloved hands. The mains power lead is retracted within the torch. Brona passes the torch to the next person in line, and it moves towards Rosie somewhere in front.

Brona strolls away in the darkness. In her coat pocket, she takes out her night-vision goggles.

'That's it, thank you, Art,' Brona hears Rosie say. 'Just plug it in there and I'll flick the switch when you're ready.'

It's the last thing she says.

Brona pauses. She takes the goggles off to look back. There is a flash. A bang, breaking glass, a pause. Disbelief and fear resonate in the interlude of silence. Then in the return to darkness, the screams start.

It is the first day. Death by light. And Brona sees it is good.

Brona returns the goggles to her eyes and makes her way through the maze of tunnels to a maintenance door several streets away.

Goggles removed, Ox-tourist gear peeled off and tucked into her coat, Brona swaps it out for the Cam equivalents. She exits into a delivery entrance on St Edmund's Passage.

She adjusts her eyes to the daylight and walks back into the crowds of demonstrators and tourists clogging up King's Parade.

She is just another speck. As she passes a shop window, she glances at herself. She is a blur in the crowd. An unseen woman in her twenties, white, average weight and height. Cambridge-Blue cap and a winter scarf masking her face. Nothing about her stands out as identifiable from thousands of others.

She's thinking about tomorrow.

She's feeling good.

Kat Latham is a three-time RITA® award-nominated author of contemporary romance. *No Man's Land* is her first crime novel, inspired partly by her grandmother's stories of the Dust Bowl and partly by her own (ungainly) attempts at roller derby. Kat is represented by Laura Bradford at Bradford Literary Agency.

kat@katlatham.com

No Man's Land
The opening of a novel

CHAPTER ONE
Oklahoma Panhandle, 1936

Centipedes scream when you burn them alive. It's an awful noise, but not the awfullest I ever heard. It's not as bad as the rattle of dirt in a person's lungs when they struggle for breath. Or the silence when a newborn baby stops cryin for the last time.

That's the worst.

But I did pity the poor centipedes as I pressed my hot iron to the wall of my home, where they burrowed and nested, and their agonized cries filled the stale air. They done nothin except try to make their home in the wrong place, and hell if that wasn't somethin I could relate to.

I lived underground then, in an abandoned dugout where my grandparents had spent their newlywed years in the last century, before they'd grew and sold enough wheat to build our beautiful home. As the name suggests, our dugout was dug straight out of the soil. Only the door and front wall was above ground. If you looked at it from far away, you'd of thought there was a door in the side of a little hill, but that hill was our roof, built from cottonwood poles and blocks of sod. When I was growin up, this was where we sheltered from tornadoes and stored our jerky.

Now it was where I lived with my husband George. Six feet underground, like prairie dogs.

Or corpses.

Not humans, anyway. Not anymore.

Just the two of us, the occasional rattler, and the bugs destroyin our walls with their tunnels till I heated the dirt around them and cooked them alive.

Our dugout was only one room, small enough to be cluttered by our necessities. Bed, table, two chairs, a potbellied stove, a lantern, and the cabinet George made to hold our tarnished silverware and cups. We had a trunk for our everyday clothes. And my pride and joy – the hope chest my Opa made me and my Oma filled for me – was at the foot of the bed. It was losin its shine by now. George used to sand and polish it for me every few years, preservin it with care. He hadn't done it since we'd moved into the dugout, and the dryness underground was takin its toll on somethin that was once filled with hope and love.

When my iron cooled off, I laid it on top of the stove till it got roastin hot again.

Our walls was covered in old newspaper to keep the dirt from fallin into the house. But behind the newspaper, centipedes and other critters dug their paths, makin a hell of a racket. Some nights I couldn't sleep because of the endless scratchin in the wall next to my head. It was a constant reminder of where I lived. How far down George and I had sunk in life.

When the iron was red-hot, I grabbed the handle with a potholder I'd crocheted with Oma when I was a child. I picked up the iron and pressed it against the newspapered wall. Steam hit the air, the small bit of moisture left in the earth reactin to the scorchin heat of the iron.

The screams followed quickly. It's a screech like you never heard in all your days, less you've had to fight insects to keep the walls from collapsin around you.

The centipedes' death cries echoed round the room as I moved the iron. I tried to block them out, but they only turned into baby cries, and that was worse yet. I sucked bits of stale air in through my clenched teeth. The iron's heat toasted my palm through the threadbare potholder, and tortured cries of dyin creatures filled my head till I'd gone round the whole room and silenced them.

No one should live so much of their life without sunlight. Without a window or fresh air. Season after season, year after year.

You wouldn't believe the things it'll do to your mind.

Here's the Plains' truth. The darkest hour don't come just before dawn. Instead it hits at noon, when the sun is shinin its brightest. When you've convinced yourself that warmth and light chased the night away for good, the storm swoops in. All you can do is try not to let it swallow you whole.

I'd finished ironin the walls and sweepin the dugout's dirt floor when George opened the door and let in the late-mornin sunlight. I blinked against the sudden brightness and smiled when I heard him whistlin 'On the Good Ship Lollypop'. My George, his face streaked with grime and his ruby-red hair slicked down with sweat, was about as far from Shirley Temple as a man could get, but that wasn't the only reason the sound made me smile. If George was whistlin, he wasn't wheezin. In that moment, his lungs was all right.

He clattered down the stairs, light in his step, and swung me into his arms, swayin side to side since there wasn't enough room for dancin. I wrapped my arms round him, ran my fingertips down his ribs. I could of counted each one, there was so little meat left on his bones, but I didn't. I'd spent plenty a night doin that as he hacked up the day's dirt. At that moment, he was swingin me round on the good ship Lollypop, and why worry about dust pneumonia in your precious few good moments?

When he got to the end of the song, he tried to dip me but stumbled. I was, it's fair to say, too much woman for him to handle anymore. But his good mood was contagious, so I laughed as I caught my balance again. 'George, what on earth's gotten into you?'

He pulled me closer and pressed his lips to my ear. 'I got a plan, Bets. A guaranteed money-maker.'

I stopped swayin. 'No.'

'Guaran-damn-teed.' His voice sounded reverent. George never met a dollar he didn't think he could turn into five. Nothin on earth was as sacred to him as the promise of a guarantee. Except I knew what these guarantees was actually worth. They was the reason I lived next door to centipedes instead of in the house I'd spent my whole life in, the one *above* the ground.

'All I need's five dollars to buy my way in, and I'll get a hundred in return, easy.'

'*Five*— ' I bit down on my tongue so hard I tasted copper. I pulled out of George's arms and turned away, but there's nowhere to go in a dugout when the sight of your husband makes you sick. Believe me, I'd tried. All I could do was shake my head and force myself to breathe.

'There's this plot of land— '

I spun around and jabbed my finger in the air. 'There's a plot of land right above our heads, George, and we used to own it till you found a guar-an-damn-teed way to lose it!'

The words bounced off the walls and slapped us both. I'd never spoke to him like that. Never flat-out accused him, even though he was the one who'd took out that awful mortgage back in 'twenty-nine. I laid a hand on his chest. It rumbled under my palm.

'I'm tryin my best to make things right,' he said, low and sad.

'I know, honey. But if we got five dollars, we're better off savin it so we can get back the land we had, not spendin it on new land that probably don't even exist.'

He wrapped his hand around mine and pressed it harder against his rattlin chest. 'It *does* exist. I seen it. Well, a drawin of it.'

'Oh, George. No, honey. No.' Hell, the closest town to us was built on fraud when we was kids. George's parents was swindled, movin all the way out here from back east, thinkin they'd bought a fertile piece of paradise on the edge of a thrivin city. They'd showed up in Boise City and found a bunch of nothin. The so-called developers didn't even own the land they was sellin. 'No more gambles. No more schemes. No more guaranteed money-makers. We save what we can, and things'll get better. They *have* to. They sure can't get worse.'

His teeth tugged at a dry scale of skin on his lower lip. I gave his hand a squeeze before lettin it go so I could run my thumb over his rough lips.

'Promise me, honey.'

His chin tipped down. 'Okay. No more guarantees.'

'You promise?'

'I just said I did, didn't I?' he groused.

'Good. Now, I made some stew. You must be hungry.'

We ate in silence but it wasn't a bad silence. More like a married-half-our-lives silence. The kind where you get lost in your own thoughts, and mine was all about the cleanin I had to do at Mrs. Richardson's that afternoon. The washin, the ironin – clothes, not walls, because she lived in a real house. Soon enough George interrupted my thoughts with, 'Bud's got a paintin job for me this afternoon. I best get ready.'

I cleared our bowls and knelt on the floor where my bucket of that day's cleanin water was. Our well was gettin dangerously low, so I had to make that water last as long as possible. I dipped a rag in it, squeezed most the water back out, and did my best to get the bowls clean. Neither of us had left much stew behind anyway. George probably would of licked the bottom clean if his tongue could stretch that far.

I heard him movin around behind me, openin our everyday trunk to get his paintin coveralls out I guessed. He was dressed in his work clothes by the time I laid the dry bowls back on the table – upside down, because so much fine dirt floated in the air that they'd fill up with filth before supper if they was right-side up. Likewise our drinkin glasses was upside down. Hell, my whole life felt topsy-turvy.

Footsteps rushed up the stairs, and I turned just in time to see the back of George as he pushed open the door.

'See you —'

The door swung shut.

'— tonight.' I pursed my lips and shook my head. What on earth was I gonna do with that man? Imagine wantin five dollars when I brought home about a dime a day from scrubbin other people's sheets with lye soap till my hands cracked and bled so bad the skin would never heal.

I took my apron off and put it in my bag to take to the Richardson's.

I *did* have five dollars, scrimped and saved over the last year, but no way in hell was I tellin George about it. That money was mine. It was a drop in the bucket compared to the mortgage and interest we owed the bank, but surely the economy would turn around soon. Even a small savings was a start to buyin back my house and my land, the place where all the people I loved best was cradled in the earth – Oma and Opa, Mama, Willa Mine. I *would* get it back, *absolutely* I would, but not if George gambled away all my chances.

I swung my bag over my shoulder and took a few steps up the stairs.

Where in the world did that silly man think he would get five dollars?

I reached for the doorknob – and froze.

No.

No no no.

I spun round and ran down the stairs so fast I near-to flew. I reached my hope chest in a few steps, fell to my knees, threw the lid open, and yanked out the spare quilt I'd made with Oma when I was a girl. More gently I pulled out my weddin dress, mold-spotted now, and the fancy weddin-night underthings that would never fit me again. I closed my eyes so I wouldn't catch a glimpse of the tiny calico dress I knew was in there too.

There, below all the fabric George would surely never paw through, was my jam jar.

I picked it up and unscrewed the lid. I turned it over.

Two coins fell out.

Nickels.

He'd left me ten cents.

'Son of a bitch,' I whispered. Not even the centipedes was around to hear me, but it didn't matter. 'You dumb son of a *bitch*.'

I shoved myself to my feet, my legs shakin so bad I could hardly stand.

'You're a dead man, George Hahn!' I shouted so loud bits of dirt fell from the ceilin and landed on my head.

I rushed out the door to catch up with him before he pissed our last money away. When I left the dugout, bright daylight scorched my eyes, and I had to shade them with my hand till I got used to it. I glanced round but George had took our car. I cursed him again. He knew I needed it to get to the

Richardsons'. Now I'd be too late for the sheets to dry and would have to ask Mrs. Richardson if I could wash them the next day, when I also had to clean the schoolhouse and the church.

I searched in all directions for a puff of dust kicked up by a car. Nothin but stillness. Any other day, I would've took the time to admire the deep-blue Oklahoma sky that stretched all the way to the earth. The kind of sky that convinced you the worst could be over. Not a whisp of a cloud, not even a whisper of a breeze to rustle the dirt. But today I didn't have the luxury.

George had said his brother Bud had some paintin job for him. Probably a lie but it was my only clue as to his whereabouts, so I took off walkin toward the road that led to town, where Bud and my best friend Pearl lived with their two kids. George and I lived in the sticks, nothin out this way except the occasional tumbledown and my own boarded-up farmhouse. To get to the town road, I walked across what used to be fields but now looked like wide, hard-baked beaches. I'm guessin that's what beaches look like, anyway. Never seen one myself. These beaches of the Panhandle are dirt, sand, and dust on top of cracked earth. The only plant you'll see for miles is tumbleweeds. It was entirely possible for a child here never to know that plants used to have roots that stuck them to the ground, rather than bein near-weightless weapons that fly through the air, claw into your flesh, and hurt like a bastard to pull out.

Nearly at the road, I stepped over a fence – easy to do because the tumbleweeds get caught there, and when the dirt rains down it piles up on top of 'em, makin little hills where folks used to fence their animals in. Fences hardly exist anymore, other than as support beams for these little hills. But maybe it don't matter anyway, because most the animals that used to be fenced in starved to death a long time ago.

A couple of jackrabbits dashed across my path, one ridin the other from behind. I thought about catchin them, but by the end of the day there would surely be one in a trap back home that I could grind up with some wheat porridge for me and George's supper. No need to carry carcasses through the swelterin heat of the day, especially when I was in a hurry.

The road was straight, flat, and covered with fine sand from the last night's winds. I trudged down the middle of it because it's easier to walk on asphalt than sand. The sun broiled my skin. I'd be burnt for sure by the time I found George, but the pink of my arms would be nothin compared to the tannin I planned to give him.

I still had a mile to go to get to Bud and Pearl's when a dot of bright silver appeared on the far horizon. The closer it got the brighter it shined, till I had to squint to keep from bein blinded. My brain picked up on the horn noise before my eyes figured out the sight, and I just barely stepped off the road in time to keep from becomin roadkill under the speedin wheels of a silver Greyhound bus.

The dirt it churned up hit me in the back of the throat, me standin there like a dodo with my shocked mouth wide open. I gagged, bent over and cursed the devil as mud dribbled out my mouth. I scraped my tongue against my front teeth to clean the layer of muck away, then wiped the spit off my chin with the back of my hand, bein careful not to get it on the sleeve of my dress. When you only got two dresses, you find yourself bein careful like that.

When I glanced up, the bus'd stopped about twenty feet after passin me. Motor still goin, it just sat there, hummin away, too far for me to see how many people was inside, if any. Too far for me to spit mud on its rear window. But not too far that I couldn't throw a rabbit carcass, if I'd of had one.

Here's the thing about Greyhound buses – they don't stop on that road. They don't even *drive* on that road. If a Greyhound bus was drivin down that road, there was only two reasons for it. One is it was lost. Two is it was up to no good.

A whole lotta nothin stretched out on either side of the road. The only breathin things along here was me, whoever was on that bus, and some fornicatin jackrabbits. I could keep walkin toward town, but that'd mean turnin my back to that bus, and somethin in my gut told me that was a bad idea.

The hair on my arms stood on end, my skin achin with nerves. Dirt skittered across the road as I stood there. The wind picked up, just a breeze at first but quickly the skirt of my dress was whippin my calves, and a sudden chill bit the air. My scalp buzzed with electricity, shootin it down to my fingertips. Only then did I notice what I'd missed because I'd been so focused on that goddamn bus. Back in the direction of home, the direction the bus was facin and I'd had my back to, a mountain range stretched for the sky.

The only mountains west of here is the Rockies, and that's some hundred miles away. This was no Father-of-Eden mountain range.

No, ma'am. This was Mother Nature's hellchild. A tidal wave of dirt and electricity barreled towards us, suffocatin anythin unlucky enough to be out in the open.

Anythin like *me*.

I ran for that bus.

And that was when the darkest hour hit.

Mother Nature blew out her lantern with a quick, rancid breath. The sun's fire was extinguished. Noon turned into midnight.

Eighteen feet. Fifteen. I ran for that bus because I knew from six long years what happened next.

'Let me in!' I screamed at the bus from ten feet away. 'Let me in!'

But the wind snatched my scream straight from my throat and shoved fistfuls of dirt in instead. I fell to my knees. Vomited a mudslide.

The earth poured down. Sand sloughed my skin raw, and tiny, sharp rocks attacked my skull, leavin craters and nicks and bloody pinpricks in my scalp. I couldn't see nothin beyond my own hands clawin the ground, but I heard plenty. The roar of the monstrous wind, *ping ping ping* of rocks bouncin hard off a metal roof.

The bus. It had to be round here somewhere. Which direction? I was curled up like a newborn protectin her hungry belly, but I was so discom-bobulated I couldn't even of told you if I was facin down or up, on my knees or on my back. Didn't matter anyhow cuz the ground was both below and on top of me, pressin on me from every which way. The bus could of been right next to me or in Timbuktu. I could of been in Oklahoma or Hell for all it mattered.

Ping.

My only chance. I moved my knees, dug my elbows, and inchwormed my way through the storm. I needed to cover my nose and mouth before I became dirt from the inside out. The bodice of my dress was too tight for me to pull it up so far, so I ripped at the hem of the skirt and pressed against my face. All I could do was try to breathe tiny breaths, to breathe without really breathin, if that makes sense.

I know it don't make sense. None of this does, if you ain't lived it.

I crawled till the pings grew louder, but the wind stole the noise and threw it all around me. Where was that goddamned bus?

A howl echoed through the wind. An animal – or me – I couldn't be sure which, and I couldn't be sure where. I kept crawlin because only one thing was certain. I was sure-as-shit not on that bus, so stayin still would kill me.

The howl came again but this time louder, which don't necessarily mean closer in a windstorm. The sound formed a word in a woman's powerful voice.

'*Lady!*'

I crawled faster, the ground rippin apart my elbows.

'La – get your hands off me I said *get* your *goddamn* hands *off me*!'

Elbow and knee, elbow and knee, breathe little little.

'She *is* out there. You saw her, sure as we all did! *Lady!*'

Words swirlin in the air, a tornado in my ears.

Just when I thought maybe it was better to stay still, curl in on myself and wait out my fate, hail burst out of the cursed sky and assaulted me with the force of George's best fastball, back when we was young. I'd once offered to catch for him but lost sight of the ball it came at me so fast, and I took the full heat of his arm right in my chest. I'd thought my heart would explode it hurt so bad. And now hundreds of ice balls slammed into me with the same force. Welts swelled on my bare arms.

My own nature took over. If I was gonna be found dead, I'd be on my feet and fightin back, not in a cower.

Never again in a cower.

One filthy hand and bit of cloth coverin my mouth and nose, I forced myself to standin and I trudged. The voice I'd heard was silenced, and I started to think I'd never heard it in the first place. Or maybe it was the voice I'd *never* heard, *her* sweet voice – the one that never got a chance to do anythin more than cry – callin me Home.

The ping of rock and ice on metal grew ferocious. The bus had to be close. If the people inside was smart, they'd have all the windows and doors shut tight. Maybe I could crawl under it, if the dirt hadn't piled up too far round the tires.

But what if it piled up after I'd crawled under? What if the bus got half buried, with me full buried under it? Was it better to be buried alive and kilt straight away in the great wide open? Or buried alive under a bus, where you might spend hours hopin for a rescue only to find the bus drivin off and flattenin you?

I reached out a hand, so desperate I wasn't thinkin straight. These dust storms was electrified. If I could see my own hair, it was sure to be wild round my head, my whole body dancin with current. I reached out and a spark lit me up inside, tossin me through the air and hard onto the earth, like a clubbed jackrabbit. My head hit the ground. Breath whooshed out, my bones explodin with pain.

Metal. I hadn't even touched it, but I'd gotten close enough.

I couldn't move. Couldn't breathe. My time had come. I laid there curled up, forehead to knees. A tiny, invisible hand wrapped itself round my finger, as it always did when I was at my most fearful. A reminder that I was not alone, will never be truly alone. Not in this world and, if God is love, not in the next neither.

I wanted to whisper her name, but my tongue was too dirt-coated and my throat too dry and swollen to get sound out. The sound of her name on the air didn't matter anyhow. It was sown in my heart and propagated through my body with every pulse.

The peltin ice-rock numbed my skin, the pain fadin to hard pressure and then nothingness. Dirt built up round me, makin me a grave that I hadn't been ready for a few minutes before. I rocked myself gently, my grave becomin a cradle, as I clutched that perfect, soft hand.

I breathed the last of the bitter air that I'd trapped between my head, belly and knees. I'd wanted to go home to my baby so desperately, and here I was about to do that. Not in the way I'd hoped. Not in the way I'd planned. But now, in that moment, I yearned for the warmth of her tiny body against mine so badly I could no longer imagine our reunion happenin any other way. As the dirt rained down on me and my thoughts slipped away, only one remained. Her weight pressed against my chest, squeezin out my last breath till my lungs was empty and my heart full again.

I don't know how it happened. I wasn't aware of anythin but a heavy weight droppin onto my curled-up back, somethin tight round my waist, and with a violent yank I was ripped away from my baby and dragged through the dirt. I gasped like a fish, my body fightin for a breath my mind didn't want me to take. I dug my battered fingers into the earth and tried to scream, tried to fight, but the tightness round my waist dug in tighter and the yanks grew sharper.

At first I thought the devil hisself had come for me. That the Lord had given me only one precious moment with Willa Mine before the prince of darkness claimed me as his own. That I would spend all eternity separated from my very heart and soul.

But soon I became aware that earthly powers had took charge of my fate. I stopped graspin at the ground and felt around my waist. A rope. My hands followed it and found another hand. All the longin in my breast seized up, and I grabbed that hand with such desperation before I realised it wasn't the one I'd been holdin moments ago. This hand was powerful. Strong and alive. Grown up. This hand was pullin the rope that was tied round my waist, draggin me through the dirt, sand and ice. This hand was tryin to save my life instead of coaxin me to the place I'd only just realised I truly wanted to be.

Gusts of wind carried the dirt here and there, and all the world was just shades of brown. But through the storm I caught glimpses of fire-red hair dancin like the devil in the air. And then the creature turned my way, and all the breath left me again. The face of a syphilitic elephant stared back at me. A monster whose body took human form but whose black, unblinkin eyes was ten times the size of a human's, whose trunk disappeared down into its human clothes.

The devil turned away, and I dug my feet into the ground, grasped at the sharp-bladed Russian thistle that blew past me. But nothin stopped the drag of my body over the earth.

Sooner than I was ready for, the pullin slowed. I blinked my muddy lids and just about made out the ghostly bus through the storm. I waited for the electric shock to knock me out. Willed it to come quickly and to stop my heart this time. But nothin doin. The hand on the rope turned into several, and they was liftin me up, all them demon faces welcomin me to Hell. I was over a shoulder, gaggin, a dusty death rattlin from my lungs.

They carried me into the bus. Laid me down in the aisle. Held my hair as I hacked and clutched at nothin but my own tore-up skin. No precious hand in mine. No sweet, soft baby skin or over-sharp baby nails. No trustin grip willin me to see her through, to fill her tummy and snuggle her to a carefree sleep.

No Willa Mine.

No nothin but eternal pain.

Shivers racked my body. That devil grief possessed me. Too bone-dry to cry. Couldn't speak. Centipede screams tore my throat jagged as I lost her all over again.

A professional journalist and copywriter, Sam writes from within the beating heart of Egoli – the City of Gold. South African born and British bred, Sam's been published on numerous platforms in multiple countries. *Kick the Tokoloshe* is Sam's first novel and Charlie Bean's first big case.

CharlieBeanMystery@gmail.com

Kick the Tokoloshe
Excerpt from a novel

Crap. I can smell crap. And fires and paraffin and rotting food.

I ease one eye half open.

It's night. The air cold and sharp and seared with smoke. The only light a flickering, half-dead streetlamp down the road.

I open the other eye.

I'm in a bath. A bath dumped at an awkward angle on a pile of trash in a field who knows where. Explains the smell. And the pain in my lower back. And why I've lost feeling in the leg currently hanging over the edge.

As I come to my senses, my body sends me a detailed list of pain, discomfort and, in my left leg, burning pins and needles. There's something squishy under my left hand. I peel it off my leg and lift it up – a hank of shocking pink hair with the roots still attached hangs limp and grim from my frozen fingers. Ugh. It's still juicy.

It being the operative word. My memories are coming back, as they usually do, in a tsunami of feelings, thoughts, images and noises. Mrs Mapondwa. Niece gone missing. Urgent call on a Sunday afternoon. Bright pink hair and outfit seen flashing through the township. Hunt through Soweto. Licking. Man, that breath. Corrugated iron slammed into the wall above my head. The Pinky Pinky was all the big noises, big bangs and big hits.

I ease myself out of the bath. My left foot isn't ready. I collapse face-first onto a rotten apple and an abandoned McDonald's box. Turns out the original owner didn't like pickle and mustard. The yellow paste slides down the vertical strands of my static-fuelled hair and oozes affectionately down my face. *There, there*, it says as it drips onto my brand-new, bright-yellow and, let's face it, magnificent leather jacket. The mustard is partly obscured by the sunny colour; the flecks of blood and splashes of pink hair are not.

I give myself a moment to take in my surroundings. How the hell did I even get here?

To my right, a barbed-wire fence lines two sides of the field with black-jacks growing thick around the edges, warring with weeds for dominance beside cement and steel. A thin path weaves up to a section of the fence that's stamped low by commuting feet, barbs biting the ground – a shortcut to a giant loop of highway that curls overhead into a junction of car farts and taxi horns. In front of me stretches a wide-open space that maybe once was green, but is now just a war between grass and shit and litter and piss.

I pull my backpack over my shoulder and tug my phone free from the side pocket. I need to call an Uber. There's a notification on my screen. Aha! I've been paid by grateful Auntie Mapondwa. It's not much, but it's enough to cover some groceries and a coffee – it looks like I managed to drop Thandi off before I passed out. I set the Uber collection point for a dirt road a few metres ahead of me, stagger upright and start walking. Well, hobbling and cursing.

I have no idea how I navigated this gathering of cinder blocks, toilet seats, rubbish bags and wiring while half unconscious. It takes me a while to get to the potholed, dusty strip of road that marks my pick-up point, but the Uber is nowhere in sight.

I reach up to touch my hair. Great. It's sticking out in all directions. I always look like I've been electrocuted after I've been in a fight. I take a moment to think enviously of the Pinky Pinky's glorious locks and freeze. Did I deliver it before I passed out, or is it still lying around somewhere? My chest tightens. I call Dr Promise.

'Charleeeee.' Delight in her voice. "Did you make it home?'

'Er.' I look around me. I'm not even sure where I am. 'No.'

'I told you, Charleee, I told you to stay here. You were grey.'

'Ah, I had to take Thandi home. You know.'

'The little one's Auntie could have collected her from here! You're too stubborn, not careful enough. Did you get her home?'

'Yeah. She's home safe, Dr Prom.'

'Eish, Charlee, stop calling me that...' A loud squawking interrupts her. 'I have to go, Charlee. I have a customer. Very bad situation. Very bad. He says his wife has been sleeping with his best friend. He's brought her in and I need to see what the chicken says. Thembi fetched the chicken from the sheds and dropped it on the floor, eish that boy, and now we must catch it. Thanks for the Pinky Pinky, by the way!'

She hangs up, but not before I catch the sounds of a furious chicken being chased in the background. Relieved, I squat down on my heels and check through my backpack. Both my Red Bulls are gone. Wow, I must have expended a lot more energy than usual this evening. Two should have kept me going until I got home. The problem is my power, ability, whatever. Dr Promise calls it the power of the ancestors, but she's got the great outfit and enormous headdress and rich heritage to pull that off. I'm so white that I could be used as an emergency beacon on a dark night. I'm not sure my ancestors are doing anything except drinking whisky in the afterlife while comparing kilt patterns.

Like all power, mine costs me. I fall over into an exhausted coma after I've expended a lot of it. Usually after I've been fighting, cursing, and, well, running. How soon the coma kicks in depends on how much energy I use, how big the fight and how many Red Bulls I drink before I get somewhere safe. I've done it often enough that I've got it almost down to a fine art. Making sure I don't fall asleep in the middle of a tussle with a supernatural, or straight afterwards, is an obsession. There's nothing as inspirational as passing out in awkward places and being found by perturbed citizens. Or pissed on by a troll.

A car comes to a dusty halt in front of me. My Uber driver has arrived.

'Eish, you drunk?' Mr White Toyota peers at my mustard and blood covered outfit. He isn't keen on me getting into his car.

'No, I was... um...' I try to think of something that won't make him drive off and leave me to walk back to my car in the cold. 'Mugged.'

He looks at the pink hair hanging in bits from my jacket and pants. 'Mugged by *tsotsis* with pink hair?'

'Yes.' I attempt to look suitably terrified and alone. He shrugs. I get in, ready to direct him to where my phone tells me that my parked car is located. I really hope it still has all its tyres.

It's five a.m. when I finally manoeuvre my battered, green Uno into Sunset Leopard, the very upmarket Sandton complex where I live. I inherited my second-floor apartment in this, the richest square mile in Africa, from my grandmother, and I fit in about as well as a crystal healer at a medical convention. My cheap-arsed piece-of-shit car surrounded by Porsches and Jaguars and Land Rovers.

Around me beats the blood of the wealthy. Here, the streets are devoid of the ankle-deep potholes that litter the rest of the city, smoothed silken by greased palms and patrolled by big men wrapped in testosterone and body armour. A multitude of private security companies surf these streets in matt-black cars branded with logos that compete for the most guns in one image. Ours is Black Widow Security. Two streets down, it's Armed

Vikings. And I'm pretty sure I saw Die Hard Security a few days ago.

As I swerve into my parking spot, I see my downstairs neighbour, Lucy Labuschagne, smothered in purple Lycra and disapproval, limbering up on the pavement beside the parking shades. She dislikes me intensely, as do a solid ninety-eight per cent of the other residents of Sunset Leopard. That's what happens when you've passed out on three different stairwells and in someone else's toilet (don't ask), and have ectoplasmic vomit on your shoes almost every time one of them bumps into you. The other two per cent is Lionel van der Byl, the muscular gym chain owner from Number 28, who thinks my reputation as local drunk and suspected prostitute is hilarious, and Ronald the gate guard, who I recently helped with his African troll issues.

Lucy's disapproval rating hits a new high as I stumble out of the car and head past her towards the stairs.

'Sies,' she manages, lips puckered tighter than I thought her fillers could manage.

'Sorry?'

She trots off down the path, a hard ignore. Ronald notices and takes a very long time to open the gate for her, ruining all her warm-up stretches as she waits in the cold. I grin. That troll was worth it.

Oh, for the love of Nutella. The door to my apartment is half open. What creature, malevolent spirit, annoyed client, or pissed-off whatever is sitting in my lounge with zero self-awareness about how movie mafia this is? I push the door wider with the tip of my takkie. It doesn't behave anything like the doors in movies. It swings back and hits my shoe.

'Ow!'

'Charlie? That you?'

'Jesus, Mak.' I march into the apartment. 'What are you doing here? And why didn't you close the bloody door? It's freezing.'

'Eish, man, sorry. I've just arrived.' Mak, perched on a bar stool beside my slate-grey kitchen bar-slash-counter, thrusts a McDonald's box at me. I'm tempted. Even with the ancient pickle smell that's formed a fast-food smog around me.

'Let me shower first.'

'Fok, what happened to your jacket? Did you fall asleep in a McDonald's? Is that *pink hair*?'

'Pinky Pinky.'

'Ahhh.' Mak nods. 'Coffee?'

'Oh, yes. Yes please.'

He heaves his muscular bulk off the stool and heads into the kitchen. Mak is enormous. Just over six foot, he has big hands and big feet and a big presence. His head, currently holding a pair of wide, black sunglasses, is bald. Mak isn't handsome – his eyes are too small and ears too big – but he's definitely arresting. I would be lying if I said I hadn't been tempted. He's sexy as hell, but he's already got four wives and they all seem permanently pissed off with him.

'It will be ready by the time you're out of the shower,' he says as he pulls the beans from the cupboard.

I turn towards the bathroom, crossing through the open-plan lounge that abuts the kitchen and two bedrooms. My apartment is cleverly designed. In spite of its relatively small size, windows and skylights make every room feel spacious. The kitchen looks like it stepped out of a home-décor magazine with grey granite countertops, white cupboards and tasteful handles. The rest of the flat is hardwood floors and pressed ceilings. I've customised my grandmother's elegant taste with two bright-orange leather sofas, a red kettle and a filter coffee machine with more knobs than a politician's office. I've also not bothered with paintings or pictures. Except two in the corner.

There used to be just one.

I slam the bathroom door shut, strip off my stinking clothes and step under the shower, not even bothering to wait for it to heat up.

A few minutes later I emerge from the bedroom, pulling a soft green jersey over a white T-shirt – there's still a nip in the winter air – and look straight at the mess of my new leather jacket draped damp over the back of the orange sofa. 'Shit.'

'It'll clean off. Leather looks better with weather.' Mak's re-established himself at the kitchen counter. 'Although nothing can make that colour better.'

Mak, real name Jim Makgotsi, is a police detective who knows precisely what I do for a living. Which is nice. Most people think I'm either making it up or making it happen. Including my old boss, the Chief of Police Koos Visser – a large, whiskery, beer boep-carrying misogynist with the personality of a tyre iron. The party he threw when I left the force was legendary. Mak showed up at my apartment afterwards, drunk as a fart and singing 'Sweet Caroline' so loudly that Lucy scuttled upstairs to yell at him, only to scuttle back down as he roared 'DA DA DAAAAAAAAAAAAAA' into her scented face mask.

'Yellow is the colour of happiness.' I smirk as I sit down next to him and grab the cup of coffee steaming beside the McDonald's he'd thrust at me earlier. I take a long, slow sip before opening the box. I blanch. 'A burger? For breakfast?'

'What?' Mak's voice is muffled as a hefty whack of syrupy pancake enters his mouth. 'It's a breakfast burger!'

I eye his McDonald's. 'Give me that.'

I cough onto his pancakes before Mak can take them back.

'You're disgusting.'

'Thanks.' My turn to sound muffled as I stuff pancake into my mouth. They're magnificent, but they need more syrup – sugar is the way to a supernatural detective's heart. 'Why're you here?'

'Nice.'

I shrug.

'Can't I just be here to visit my friend?'

I stop chewing and stare at him.

'Fine, fine. I've got something for you. A crazed killer with a possible Charlie twist.'

'Tell me more.'

Mak leans back against the kitchen wall. 'So far, we've got three bodies, washed up on the spruit wrapped in white industrial webbing. Two members of the local Zionist church found the bodies yesterday after they'd gone for a walk upstream to find out why their people were getting sick after baptism. Turns out they'd been taking in bits of dead body along with Jesus.'

'No, man.'

'Ja, and they've been twisted into pretzel shapes, like this.' Mak puts his left arm behind his back and his right across his chest, twisting both shoulders to mimic a grotesque mummy. 'They're with Kerry at the moment to assess time and cause of death.'

Kerry Lancaster's the forensic pathologist who works with Mak at the Gauteng Violent Crime Unit (GVCU), a public-private partnership between the South African Police Services (SAPS) and a conglomerate of private security companies headed up by Angry Badger Security. It's an experimental, state-of-the-art crime unit designed to bypass bureaucracy and incompetence using the best-of-the-best of people, technology and systems to actually catch criminals.

'Has she found anything yet?' I ask.

'It's very weird. The three bodies have been folded into the same position and held in place by the same webbing, and they're all missing their hearts.'

'Seriously? Their hearts?'

'Ja, and...' Mak pauses. 'They stink. Like shit. Animal shit. And are covered in scratches, bites and gouge marks.'

'That's... odd. But still could be some nutter eating his way through his victims. We've seen weirder. I'm not seeing the connection to my, um, skills.'

'We found cat bones tied with hair pushed into the heart cavities.'

'Right, that'll do it.' That last fact, added to the missing hearts, has moved the conversation straight into my territory. The land of the supernatural weird and wonderful.

'The pressure on this one has been fast and strange, Charlie. We got the call from the priests early yesterday morning and, while the last body was being loaded into the van, one of the bigwigs was on the phone to the Chief. Fix it, and fix it fast. Use any means necessary. He was like an angry ferret after that, poking into everyone's business, tramping all over the crime scene.'

Chief Visser, the asshat I lovingly call Chief Kak, heads the GVCU and reports to Jonas Kinwasi, Director General of the SAPS, and Barbara McGovern, CEO of Angry Badger Security. The GVCU has an impressive success rate because it can afford people like Kerry and Mak and Ebrahim Lovejoy – possibly the best detective ever born – but its funding structure means hierarchy, key performance indicators and metrics. The Chief is more pencil pusher and goalpost achiever than detective.

'Chief was twitchy, Charlie. When Kerry showed him the cat bones, he told me to get you in. Payment guaranteed.'

Wait, what?

'Payment?' I'm not sure that the word really captures the full scale of my *Holy crap, what are you saying?*

Mak shifts. It's clear that this is the part of the conversation he wasn't looking forward to. 'Eish, Charlie. I know you don't want to work for him again – it's a mess after everything that happened. But payment...'

Mak knows I'm broke. After all, the reason I'm now a freelance detective slash supernatural hunter slash stopper of all things nasty is because of the incident that cost me my job and my reputation. After everything went down, Chief Kak made it his life's mission to create a working environment so toxic that I'd show myself the door. He was successful. Me, on the other hand, not so much. My salary is sporadic financial gratitude from terrified Joburg citizens sent my way by Dr Promise and her network of sangomas.

'How much?'

'The Chief says that you can have your fee of six-hundred rand an hour, no questions asked. Until you give us a verdict. Then, he will decide what happens.'

'Wait, what?'

Mak winces. 'Ja, so your job is to decide what kind of "fokken strange kak" this is and then he'll bring in someone to deal with it.'

'Are you serious?'

'He doesn't trust you, Charlie. After what happened with Fiona...'

My old partner, killed in the line of duty. Everyone blamed me. Nobody knew what really happened that night. Except me, Mak and Dr Prom.

'That was not my fault. Nobody could've predicted that. Nobody.' I'm fierce with remembered rage.

'That night he saw things,' Mak says. 'I don't think he understands what he saw. He needed someone to blame. He's not all bad, Charlie. He's just...'

'A knob.' I helpfully finish for him. 'What happened to cops stand together, Mak?'

Mak sighs. I shake my head. There's no point. I hate and blame myself as much as Chief Kak does. 'He also said you'll get clearance – expert-advisor status.'

'Huh.' That's going to be interesting. I've not been back to the GVCU since I left a year ago. The thought fills me with a mix of dread and excitement.

'It'll be good to have you back. Have you at my back.' Mak says. 'You've been missed by those who count.'

I attempt a smile. Mak looks concerned, inching away. 'Do you have gas?'

I glare at him. Then look down at my congealed pancakes. They've lost their appeal. I stand up and start tidying away the fast food and cold coffee cups.

'We've seen some weird shit over the years, all of us,' Mak says, sounding worried. 'We all know that your world exists, but nobody ever says a word. It's just this thing, over there. Those of us who know, we call the right people. Used to be the local sangomas, now it's you. The Chief obviously knows I tell you when we hit a case that fits so you can get private pay to fix the problem, but he never says a word to me or anyone else. Then he has that call yesterday and he turns white – hehe, whiter – and tells me to pull you in.'

'Who called him?'

'I think it's either Jonas or Barbara. But why would one of them get involved?'

'I've got a funny feeling, Mak.'

'Could be the pancakes. Stolen food makes you sick.'

'Har har, very funny.' I wave his empty coffee cup at him. 'More?'

'Please.'

I pour the last of the coffee and top up our mugs with a splash of milk. I slide the sugar over to Mak – he's not keen on sugar-free – and take a slow sip. I fetch my jacket and bring it into the kitchen, putting it on the metal draining board. Mak, used to how I process things, opens up his phone and starts reading his messages. It looks tiny in his hands.

I open a drawer under the sink and pull out my leather-cleaning kit. Leather cleaner is a business essential in my line of work because leather is my single most important weapon. It's the only material that can be used to capture and hold the supernatural, and it forms a natural shield, protecting me from supernatural smacks. The cleaner and more supple it is, the better it works. Dr Prom's mantra 'The cleaner the leather, the better' was drilled into me from the very first lesson.

I remove most of the hairs, pickle and sauce from the jacket with a paper towel, then, using soapy water and a sponge, I gently wash away the stubborn sticky stuff. I use another cloth to wipe the jacket dry and then rub in the leather conditioner, the delicious lemon scent proving a bonus in getting rid of the Pinky Pinky stink.

'How do you think the bodies got to the spruit?' I ask, as I massage in the last bits of beeswax. 'You think maybe the storm on Thursday night shook them loose from somewhere?

'Ja, that's a possibility. That storm was a doozy.'

It was also completely out of season and unnatural. I've been on edge ever since.

'Neighbouring complex caught fire,' I say. 'The lightning hit that gigantic palm tree.'

'Shit, did the fire get far?'

'Nah, with all the money in this area, the fire brigade actually arrived.'

Mak laughs.

'Okay, so the bodies. Just three? None higher up or further down the spruit?' I ask.

'Ebrahim thinks there are more, somewhere. You know his...'

'...hyena senses,' I finish. We both grin. Ebrahim is an exceptional detective and one of the people I miss working with the most since being forced out of the, well, force. His 'hyena senses' are famous. He's got a knack for finding information and clues in places where everybody else has already looked.

'Ja, so, Ebrahim checked the river and surrounding area and can't find anything. It's not surprising. That storm destroyed half the indigent camps, and a few of the houses nearby have trees instead of walls. The bodies could have come from anywhere. A camp. A house. Hell, just dumped.'

'Where were they found?'

'Up near Chateaux Gateaux, just down from the Scout Hall.'

Mak's referring to the part of the spruit that weaves alongside some of the wealthiest homes in Johannesburg, where the rich and skinny cycle along a verdant path beside litter-decorated water.

'Do we know who's wrapped in the webbing yet?'

'Kerry said she'd message me as soon as she finds out, but it's going to be a while yet.'

Yeah, South Africa. If it's not admin in triplicate, it's unnecessary delays and long waits. Police work has to be a calling, otherwise you'll be a gibbering wreck by the end of month two.

'Nobody's at the scene now...' Mak looks at me. 'Come, if we go now, you can take a look around before Ebrahim does another sweep of the area. It could help.'

I'm torn. I did get some sleep in the bathtub, but that wasn't enough and I'm shattered.

'Erk.'

Mak shakes his head. 'This could be your only chance to see if you can pick up anything from, you know, your side.'

He's right. The police know how to avoid ruining forensic evidence – well, mostly – but have a tendency to trample right over evidence that can help me figure things out from the supernatural perspective. This often slows me down. It also drives me nuts.

'Okay, let me get ready.'

I grab my backpack and stuff it full of anti-nasty sprays, three Red Bulls and some extra leather strips. I also use the leather cloth to wipe off a couple of bloodied pink hairs from one of the straps.

'Let's go,' I say as I throw on my now-gleaming yellow leather jacket.

'Do you have to wear that?'

CHAPTER TWO: GARY

This case smells as bad as the half-sludge, half-water of the Braamfontein Spruit that's currently lapping at the toes of my takkies. The stream is a dustbin of cans, plastic bags, excrement, soap suds and takeout boxes.

Fed by the storm on Thursday night, the spruit has picked up speed and plenty of trash from the indigent communities living beside the river in shacks made of cardboard boxes and stolen road signs. These collapsible shelters housing hundreds are rammed up beside the ten-foot, electricity- and alarm-protected walls of the Bryanston wealthy. A juxtaposition that defines Johannesburg – from the townships without power cuddled up to Sandton's connected wealth, to the walking gogos beside luxury sedans driven by teens.

I can hear an insistent 'tick, tick, tick, tick, tick' coming from my right. A tree has fallen onto the remains of a nearby wall, branches pressing down on the wires of the electric fencing that once ran along the top, creating a tangled, ticking mess.

'The bodies were there?' I point at some jagged rocks running across the narrow watercourse. Two yoghurt tubs battle for freedom. One makes a break for it and is whisked away by the current.

'Ja.'

I sniff.

'I can still smell something rotten.'

'Yebo, the smell from the bodies was something else. They had been rotting in the water for a few days at the least. It wasn't helped by the storm churning out all this litter and kak either.'

'Yeah, this is a mess.'

'Thing is,' Mak continues, 'Kerry said, from her first cursory examina- tion, that the decay indicated they were kept somewhere cold. She started talking about the effects of the varied temperatures of the Joburg winter on decomposition stages.'

'Oh? And? What did she say?'

'I left.'

Mak the scientist.

'Could they have been killed recently?'

'Again, no idea. Kerry's holding a briefing tomorrow. Hopefully she'll have something for us.'

I give him a look.

'Yes, yes, I will pass on all the information she gives us. Although we're hoping your clearance will come through today so you can join us.'

'Seriously?'

'Ja, the Chief said you're in for everything except the stuff that's none of your business.'

'Loosely translated as – until he decides I know enough.'

'Probably.' Mak shrugs. 'The problem is that we don't have any clues about where they could have come from. The spruit is too blocked for them to come from upriver, by the Pick n Pay on Thyme, and nobody would have missed bodies lying on the path or in the bushes for the past however many days. It's like they've come from nowhere.'

'Or they were dumped.'

'Or they were dumped,' Mak agrees. 'They can't have come from far, though.'

'Why?'

'Webbing was still too tight and too neat. The bodies were covered in mud and sticks, but all of it was fresh, added by the storm and the flotsam of the spruit, not ingrained, like it would've been if they'd been buried or dragged. When we pulled them out the water they just looked, you know, new. Someone had to have carried them here.'

A horn blares. We both jump. Mak's bloody ringtone.

'Yebo?' Mak wanders off to answer his phone. I squat down by the river's edge, something teasing at the edge of my senses.

Mak appears at my right shoulder. 'I have to go. Chief wants me back at HQ for a debriefing. You've probably got about twenty minutes here before the team comes in for another sweep. Try not to let them see you. We've not made you official yet, and without me here you'll just get into trouble.'

I grimace. 'No problem. I won't be long.'

Mak pats me on the shoulder and saunters back up the path, ducking beneath the yellow crime tape wrapped around the trees to stop people from entering the scene. Not that it makes any difference in Joburg. Most of the tape will be stolen by lunchtime.

I press my hands into the soil. Waiting. Something is here. I cock my head. The smell is worse. I take a deep breath, and gag.

Fresh Tokoloshe spoor.

Tokoloshe are all the adjectives used to describe an evil creature. Almost at the top of the terror totem pole, these supernaturals are strong, violent and feral. Usually summoned by a truly nasty piece of humanity who has zero interest in human kindness, Tokoloshe are tools used to intimidate people, to take control of territory, or to get revenge. Summoners are the kind of people who wallow in dark emotions and evil intentions, enjoying the power of these one-creature murder units without getting blood anywhere near their own hands. They use Tokoloshe as other people would use a whisk – to beat the shit out of anything they want.

One of the signs that a Tokoloshe has been in the area is the smell.

Tokoloshe can shapeshift into cats, dogs or primates, and they shit when they shift – they can't help it. And a Tokoloshe just shifted. Now.

I go cold. I can't catch a Tokoloshe alone.

Thing is, I can't just leave it here. There are police coming. People live here. I need to find it. Especially if this is the creature that's murdering all these people. Anyone in its path is in danger.

'*Lalela.*' I say the word for 'listen'. I close my eyes. My enhanced hearing catches every sound and scratching insect in the vicinity.

Trickle. Splash. Tick. Tick. Tick. Water, stream, electric fence.

Crack. Hum. Roar. Belch. Taxi backfiring, early morning traffic.

Skitter. Scratch. Hiss. Beetles, bugs, wind.

Purr. Purr. Patter. Pad. A cat.

No, not a cat. A tokoloshe.

I spin and run straight towards the sound of the creature padding through the trees.

Rebecca Marchant is a lifelong writer with a passion for therapeutic writing, the supernatural and subverting tired tropes. Her former work as a graphic artist, academic, and NGO administrator has informed her latest novel, set in contemporary Norwich and drawing on the dark history and folklore of the city.

evenlode1967@gmail.com

Maddermarket
The opening of a paranormal crime novel

PROLOGUE
Norwich, Autumn 2018

Something is moving under the skin of the city.

Even before the unseasonal fog creeps in from the north coast, there is a crawling under the paving slabs. The grass in Eaton Park is groaning into new shapes, hummocks and depressions like the twists of a scoliotic spine where the lawns were once smooth as billiard tables. Bulbs poke out gnarled, deformed shoots. There's a strange hum amongst the bare branches of the trees up on Mousehold Heath, where the brambles lash out at passersby. The rooks that flock in their hundreds over the university campus grow hoarse and frantic as they wheel in their evening susurration over the packed car parks. There is a shiver in the limes down on the Earlham Road, and the water in the River Wensum trembles in anticipation of something no one can quite name.

The children in the school yards are listless, their legs leaden, their shrieks muted. They are afraid to make too much noise, in case something in the air notices them. The shopping malls echo to few footsteps. The shoppers are sparse and apathetic. The voice of the busker under the porch in London Street is tremulous, and no one has seen the Puppet Man, the city's favourite eccentric, in weeks. Amongst the stalls on the market, under the awnings, the regulars queue up for their lunchtime bacon sandwiches and hot teas with grey faces, hunched and watchful. No one is buying fancy cakes or cheeses. The city has lost its appetite.

Pregnant women turn up at doctors' surgeries with flipping, swooping foetuses, and old ladies break out in unexplained hives. Toddlers cry from a buzzing in their ears that keeps them awake at night, making their mothers frantic with exhaustion. Washing machines leak and water mains explode. In darkness, the air crackles with static, making the televisions snowy and the sleepers restless. The sky is leaden, inanimate.

The ground underfoot is waiting.

CHAPTER ONE
The first Saturday

It was getting dark when Dr Peter Mothersole left the cathedral library. The days were shortening and the twilight down in the cloister had a pinkish quality. He could hear the roar of the crowd downriver at the Carrow Road football ground. The muffled sound bounced off the ancient stones as he made his way back toward the nave. He couldn't remember who City were playing this week, but it sounded like it was going well – there would be a lot of happily full pubs tonight.

The nave was warm and bright. Candles flickered in silver candlesticks on the central altar, their soft light a reminder that Christmas was only weeks away. Little snippets of conversation, whispers of life, echoed around every arch and pillar. It was near closing time, and only a few visitors lingered. He was not sure if the whispers were from them, or from older congregants, long passed souls drawn home to the shadowy corners and the worn pews. At this time of night, it was easy to believe the cathedral itself was whispering.

The air outside was sharp. There had been a wind when he left home, but it had died down. The cold gnawed at his nose. He pulled his jacket around him, hunched up. Time to dig out the winter coat. His faithful tweed wasn't going to cut it much longer.

He had gone a few paces across the cobbles, towards the Erpingham Gate when his legs started slowing him down, growing heavier. And there it was, that familiar tang of tin. He stopped to sniff the air, and an old woman trudging by, wheeling a shopping trolly behind her, gave him a funny look.

There are two things that smell like tin to a witch: blood and magic. And he knew them both only too well.

His scalp started to prickle.

Something was coming.

He turned back, drawn to the other end of the Cathedral Close by the scent. He followed it as it grew stronger, round the corner of the choir school buildings. From there, even in the gloaming, he could see the arch of Pulls Ferry at the bottom of the lane, the little gatehouse from which a ferryman used to punt passengers across the River Wensum for a few coins. There was a streetlamp on the other side of the archway to light pedestrians using the riverside walk. He could see the stalk of the lamp, and the lurid glow of the bulb. Traffic roared on the opposite bank, cars full of families heading home from shopping, or towards Riverside to the cinema, bowling alley and restaurants.

The water was hard to see, and it was not because the light was bad.

A mist was crawling up the slipway towards it, low and white, like a creeping animal. It had already smothered the glitter of the river behind it, and now it was slithering towards the Cathedral Close, towards the city's heart, towards him.

He turned on his heel and ran.

There was a huge window in the top-most front room of the house that Peter shared. It took up almost the whole of the wall, and looked down onto Tombland, the street where the main traffic passed the entrance to the Cathedral Close. Like the rest of the house, the window was crooked, the wooden mullions lurching drunkenly. In fact, there was nothing straight about the house at all. It was rickety and misshapen, all creaking timbers, lath and plaster, without a truly level beam or floorboard in the whole structure. Both outside and inside, it gave the impression of a house of cards, vertical and horizontal planes leaning at angles with a tenuous stability that belied its five hundred year history. 'On the Huh' was how the Norfolk people put it, and they were right. The house was like everything else in Peter's life, a shambles held together by hope and habit. It was rented, complete with ghosts, from the Diocese.

Peter's housemate, Alf, was sitting in the big window, watching for him. Peter spotted him as he approached, his face pale in the light of the busy street. He looked even more drawn than usual. As soon as he saw Peter, he whipped away from his eyrie, and Peter knew he was in for it. When he let himself in and staggered up the stairs, breathless, he was not surprised to find Alf waiting at the top, wound tight, arms wrapped around his body.

'Where the hell have you been,' he demanded as Peter pushed past him, panting from his mad dash. He flung his satchel on to the kitchen table and pulled off his jacket, trying to get his breath back.

'Where's the hagiometer?'

Alf came up behind him. 'In the workshop. I've been making a few adjustments.'

'It's working, though, isn't it? Please tell me it's working?'

'Please tell me you brought my dinner,' Alf countered, and Peter could see the desperate look in his eyes.

He pulled the plastic bag out of the satchel. 'The butcher said he put something special in for you tonight. Heart. He knows you like that.'

Alf groaned with relief and grabbed the bag from Peter's hand. He pressed its opening to his face, over his nose, and inhaled. Peter caught a whiff of the raw meat.

'I'll leave you to it,' he said, picking up the satchel again because he needed all his notes from it.

Alf looked up at him, and nodded. His blue eyes were sharp with hunger. Peter closed the door, and took the next flight of stairs two at a time.

Up at the top, in the storey that jutted out over the busy pavement, was Alf's workshop. Peter switched on the light, and tools and instruments gleamed, each in its place. Not that Alf was obsessively tidy; the state of his bedroom gave that away. It was just that the kind of work he did required meticulous organisation as well as precision. His workbench was an ancient slab of oak, worn and pitted. It was shaped in a semicircle to accommodate his chair, and beneath it was the familiar bank of tools, hasps, miniature saws, tweezers, clamps, and irons that were the meat and drink of his trade. On top were dozens of small plastic and metal trays, lined up in careful rows. Some were recent buys from the old-fashioned hardware shop in Exchange Street where the shop assistants still wore brown overalls and knew Alf by name. Some he had owned for years. Some looked old enough, and cracked enough, to have been inherited. Each one contained tiny cogs, posts, gears, screws, all of brass, sorted in order. He had been taking a clock apart, and if the order got mixed up, he might not be able to put the mechanism back together. A few of the more delicate components of the clockwork system were laid out on rectangles of green baize. More were soaking in a bath of chemicals that could lift away the accumulated sludge of the years. The only bit Peter could identify was the clock face itself, made of enamelled brass, looking like a fish out of water without its hands or housing. He could just about read a number on the worn, waxy white enamel: 'London 1779'. Hence why Alf was taking his time, doing it by the book. It was going to be beautiful when he had finished.

The wall to the left of the bench was hung with larger tools: hand drills, saws, screwdrivers, cutters and nippers, and other, more specialised gear with ancient names that Peter didn't know. There were ranks of tiny drawers, labelled in Alf's neat copperplate. An old wire basket was full of folded blueprints. The back wall was where the machines sat, the lathe Alf had built himself, all kinds of electric saws and drills. The whole room smelled of metal and solder and oil, the odour of Alf himself. This was what invention smells like, Peter had come to realise.

On top of cupboards, along with a dozen or more ancient clocks, large and small brass objects clicked and spun and whirred, highly polished cogs and gears glittering, the fruit of Alf's labours, the children he would never have. Peter stopped for a moment and listened. It felt as if the whole house was ticking, the seconds and minutes being marked, sliced off Time, as if the ancient oak beams throbbed to the pulse of the endless flow of the hours.

And there, in the midst of it all, was the polished walnut box that contained the heartbeat of Peter's work. The hagiometer that Alf had made for him.

He opened the lid, carefully. It sat inside on its bed of green velvet, looking innocently like a brass ship's clock. He would need to recalibrate it if Alf had been fiddling with it, but it was such a sleek machine that it would only take a few minutes. The old one used to take days. That was how good Alf was. Which was lucky because, when Peter glanced out of the window, he could see that mist was beginning to skim along the pavements, as if the flagstones were steaming.

Whatever it was, it was coming soon. There was no time to waste.

When he turned around, Alf was standing on the threshold, leaning against the doorframe. He looked even paler than before, though there was a slight flush on his razor-sharp cheekbones and an unnatural brightness in his eye that spoke volumes.

'All done?' Peter asked as he closed the lid of the box and tucked it under his arm.

Alf nodded, then seemed distracted. Something outside had caught his attention, and he drifted towards the window.

'Are you okay?' Peter asked him.

Living with someone like Alf was handy. He was like human seaweed. He knew which way the wind was blowing, and not just in meteorological terms. Peter had his senses, his genetic talents, but it was good to have Alf around to prove to him that he was not just imagining things. That he was not imagining things tonight, in particular.

They stood side by side at the window, looking down. Taxis were starting to gather around the clump of trees close to the far gate, and the restaurants and cafes on the other side of the street were lighting up, preparing for the first rush of business of the evening. The air was thickening, and not just because of the mist. Peter glanced at Alf, and saw his hand flutter to his throat, long bony fingers plucking at the scarf he always wore to hide his skin. Peter could see he was trembling very, very slightly.

'What is it?' He whispered, hardly daring to allow his voice to disrupt the sound of his breathing, or the clicking and whirring of the machines.

Alf swallowed.

'Mist,' he said.

'It's coming up from the river,' Peter told him. 'I saw it when I came out of the cathedral. And I smelled tin.'

Alf gave Peter a look like a knife, pupils dilating. Then swiftly turned away and tapped the barometer he kept by the window with his knuckle.

'Fog isn't usual for this time of year,' he said, examining the reading, suddenly all business. He opened a little notebook and scribbled numbers down at the bottom of a column. 'December, January, perhaps, but it's too early yet. And the barometer is too low. We should be expecting rain, not mist.'

'So?' Peter wanted his conclusions, to know if he could taste the same thing on the evening air.

He looked at Peter with that intense gaze of his. His hands fluttered to his throat again.

'He's coming,' he breathed.

'Who is coming?'

He turned away and made for the door.

'Alf!' Peter called after him. Alf hesitated, looked down into his eyes as they paused in the doorway.

'You need to lock me in,' he said.

Peter looked at his chest and brushed at the cloth of his shirt with his finger.

'You got your dinner down your front,' he said.

A few drops of blood, there, on the pristine white cotton.

'There's no time,' Alf said, and Peter caught that familiar whiff of tin on his breath.

'Come on,' he said. 'Let's get you settled down.'

THE FIRST SUNDAY
Sally

Sally Jessett let herself in through the back door of her Hethersett home, her running shoes shedding muddy crumbs on the kitchen floor. The fog had left a dew on her skin. She could still feel it clinging to the insides of her lungs. She caught sight of her reflection in the glass front of one of the cabinets, dark hair stringy with moisture and sweat, sweatshirt dank and humid. The cat sauntered up and tangled around her legs as she tried to unlace her shoes.

'Out of the way,' Sally huffed.

The cat looked up at her, doing the big eyes routine.

'I fed you before I went out, so don't try that one on me!' Sally told her.

The cat was adamant she had not eaten in at least three weeks. In the end, Sally threw a handful of cat crunchies into the bowl before the beast tripped her up so that she cracked her head open on the corner of the washing machine, and died there on the lino.

'And don't come crying for more.'

The cat, who was incongruously named Dave, did not bother to look up from her bowl. She was ghostly white and female, despite the moniker. Dave was originally called Hermione, but Sally quickly discovered she felt a complete idiot shouting 'Hermione!' at the back door whilst banging a spoon against the base of a plastic cat bowl. Chris had suggested 'Dave' because it was shorter and less embarrassing to shout. He seemed oblivious to the fact of Dave's gender. Ease of use, however, made the name stick. The cat remained Dave, though Chris had since messily departed.

Sally heard the Sunday papers being thrust through the front door. They dropped with a heavy thud onto the carpet. She flung open the fridge and pulled out the orange juice, slugged it straight from the plastic bottle because there had to be some compensations for singledom, and glugging juice from the bottle when you were thirsty had better be one of them. She was still trying to catch her breath, even after her warm down.

She tossed a pod into the coffee machine, lined up a mug and pressed the button, then checked her phone.

Voicemail.

Sally and her team had wrapped up a major domestic violence case on Friday, and her superior officer, Commander Hopkins, said that to be fair, she ought to be off the duty rota for the weekend as reward. But life is not fair, as her everyday work taught her long ago.

She pressed the green button.

It was Chloe, her deputy SIO, on the way to a new crime scene. She could hear the drone of the car engine in the background, the ticking of the indicator as Chloe turned a corner.

'Morning Guv. Sorry to raise you from the dead so early on this gorgeous morning, but we've got a murder,' she said. 'Meet me down at Bishop's Bridge in the city. Ackland was the duty officer, so we're off to a good start. See you soon.'

Sunday morning, not even nine o'clock. Here we go again.

Sally took her coffee off the machine and added some milk. She calculated that she could have a quick shower, grab a bowl of cereal, throw together some sandwiches and get out of the door in less than half an hour if she got a shimmy on. So much for reading the papers.

Dave the cat had finished her crunchies. She blinked up at Sally, licking her chops ostentatiously.

'It's alright for some,' Sally grumbled.

Sally parked at the bottom of Bishopsgate, by the old Red Lion pub, its boarded-up windows blindly facing the ancient Bishop's Bridge over the Wensum. The uniformed police had commandeered the pub's car park as the best place to leave vehicles, and Sally pulled up behind a forensics van and climbed out. A blue and white tape had been draped across the riverside walk opposite, between the houses that bordered the officially designated footpath. It was tied to the robust iron gates that shut the walkway off at night. The line was being guarded by a rather whey-faced young ranker who was hovering on the balls of his feet in an effort to keep warm. He had obviously already learned that on days like these, if you didn't keep moving, your boots could freeze to the pavement.

Sally remembered those days all too well. Chilblains and constant colds and pulling drunks off each other's throats. The joys of community policing. Thank God for CID.

She pulled her wellingtons out of the car boot and put them on, then locked her handbag in and set off for the fray.

The fog lay heavily over the banks of the river, shrouding the shallow slope on the far side. She knew this place had a dark history, and it was easy to fancy she could still see a whisp of smoke from the dell opposite where they used to burn heretics on wretchedly bitter mornings just like this.

DS Chloe Merton met her in the alley where the footpath threaded between high walls of residential gardens. She was hunched into her padded parka, the hood pulled up over the beautifully balayaged blonde of her hair, the thermal layers making her look twice as large as her usual, ample size. Her face was pinched red by the cold.

'Morning, Guv.'

'Morning Chlo. Lovely weather for it.'

'Isn't it just grand,' Chloe grimaced. There was a dewdrop hanging from the tip of her nose, and she dashed it off with the back of her hand in irritation.

They set off along the riverside path. Recent storms had created bedlam along the riverbank, tearing the last of the copper leaves off the trees and banking them up against streetlamps and fence panels. They had to negotiate several enormous puddles.

'Alright, what have we got?'

'White female, late teens, maybe early twenties, naked, no belongings, no phone, no real sign of cause of death, and no sign of a struggle.'

'Oh, great,' Sally huffed, and her breath made a cloud in the sharp morning air. 'Plenty to go on then.'

They stopped to pull on their footsies at the perimeter of the designated search zone, weaving their way between the various forensics officers carefully marking items lying on the pavement.

'The body was found on a pontoon just behind the school boathouses,' Chloe went on. 'The access to the bank is almost nil; you have to go through the boathouse door, but that's been locked for months according to forensics. Or there's a small path through the undergrowth, but that's waterlogged at the moment.'

'Footprints?'

Chloe shook her head. 'The mud is so mushed up that it's impossible to see.'

'Maybe she was dumped from the river then?'

'Can't tell at this point,' Chloe said, as they rounded the end of the high wall and came onto an apron of concrete in front of a low, wide building. One storey, it did not look very well kept, and only had one door, painted blue, and a couple of windows, one either side, each double-glazed with an inner skin of spider's webs. Drab silver birches and willows overhung the area, dripping miserably onto the concrete, and flaking the last of their leaves like dead skin.

A man emerged from behind the righthand side of the building, where the trees were thickest. He was one of many wearing the white forensic suits, but Sally recognised his balding head and cadaverous features as Sam Acland, the duty DI who had taken the call when it first came in. It was Sam she would be reliant on for the accurate management and recording of the scene.

'Morning, Ma'am,' he said. 'Bit of a puzzler, this one.'

'Can we go through the boathouse?'

He shook his head. 'Sorry, haven't managed to track down the caretaker who has the keys yet, but I've got two officers working on it right now. In the meantime, we'll have to go down over the bank. Good thing you brought your wellies. The kit's over here.'

Sally and Chloe put on the white paper suits he pulled from a kitbag left by the wall and followed him through the undergrowth down the side of the boathouse. There were a lot of tangled brambles to wade through, with bits of litter that looked like dirty rags caught in them.

'Any traffic on the river last night, Sam?' Sally called to him as he led the way.

'Not likely in that weather. You could have cut it with a knife!' He had reached the edge of the water and was holding his arms out from his sides to balance on the muddy slope.

'Chloe, check with the Broads Authority and the cruiser companies,' Sally said, turning round. Chloe was looking uncertainly at the slippery surface, and then at her feet. Whatever grip her boots had would not function through the footsies.

'Erm,' she said.

'Come on, Chlo,' Sally said, holding out her hand to steady her deputy. 'No one'll see if you fall on your arse here.'

Chloe reached out. 'I'm more worried about falling in the river.'

They managed to shuffle through the mud to a place where willow wattles had been put down to stabilise the bank. From there, it was a short stride across a foot or so of water onto the pontoon.

Now Sally got a better view of the river. Everything was shrouded in chilling grey mist. It lay on the surface of the water and clung to the treetops. There were two dilapidated houseboats moored further down, close to the Foundry Bridge, but she could see no sign of Broads cruisers or other boats, and it was impossible to make out the looming Victorian monolith of the railway station on the other side.

'Someone could have rowed across from the other side,' Chloe said, standing next to her on the wooden slats. The pontoon was covered in what looked like thick plastic sheeting, shredded in places, and nailed down to wooden boards stained black with wet and mould. If this structure belonged to the cathedral school, it was unusually badly maintained. Sally knew the fees for their pupils were high, and they generally kept their premises in top condition.

Two forensics officers were finishing rigging up screens to hide the pontoon from the opposite bank, where a few people were already gathering in the mist, indistinct grey shapes milling around, forming the usual ghoulish audience. The shape of the platform made it unsuitable for the usual protective tents, so it was necessary to protect the scene some other way. There was not much room to stand, so Acland ordered his staff off temporarily so that Chloe and Sally could survey the scene.

In the middle of the pontoon stretched the pale form of the girl. Sally stepped up to look, feeling the familiar sensation of her guts flipping. The scent of rotting vegetation, dank river mud and ice-cold air clung to her nostrils.

The girl lay with her upper body and shoulders flat on the board, twisted at the waist, her hips and legs turned to the left, her knees drawn up a little. Her arms were flung out to either side. Her skin had the blue tinge of dead flesh. Her hair, dulled by the bitter night and the damp, fanned out around her head in a straw-coloured halo. Her face looked peaceful.

Sally crouched down to look more closely.

No scars or track marks in the obvious places, so not a drug user, at least not the injecting kind. She looked plump, well-fed. A few leaves and burrs in her hair. No lividity. Now that *was* odd.

'How long has she been here, do we reckon?'

'I'd say she died between 1am and 3am from the liver temperature,' said a woman's voice, and turning her head, Sally saw the plump, familiar shape of Dr Christina Clarke, the duty medical officer, stepping onto the pontoon. 'Sorry, had to get something from the car.'

Sally looked at the body again. 'Cause of death?'

'Not obvious,' Dr Clarke said, fiddling with the packet she had in her latex-gloved hands.

'At a guess?'

She made a face. 'I'd say she bled out, but if she did, it wasn't here.'

Sally looked for a wound, but could not see one, just what looked like bites on the girl's neck.

'Where did she bleed from?'

'The neck, I assume, but it's a small wound. Bit of a poser. I'll leave it to the pathologist, I think. I can only give you the basics of what I see.'

'So, we're looking at this as a deposition site rather than a murder scene?'

'I should say so, wouldn't you? I can't see anywhere round here where a healthy young woman has lost ten pints of blood in the last 12 hours.'

Sally was looking at a smear on the girl's soft belly, something red and slightly gritty wiped across it, as if with the palm of a hand.

'What's this,' she asked, pointing.

'Looks like paprika,' Chloe said, peering over her shoulder.

'No idea,' Dr Clarke said. She had managed to pull a pack of swabs out of the packet she had been wrestling with. 'Not familiar to me. Looks vegetal, but that's all I can tell you. Can I get on?'

Sally and Chloe stood back so that she could crouch down by the body and set to work again. They watched her swipe a swab through the red smear for a few moments before Chloe spoke.

'No ligature marks on the wrists or ankles.'

'No,' said Sally.

'How does a healthy girl bleed out from such a small wound? It doesn't look deep enough.'

'Carotid artery, sergeant,' Dr Clarke said. 'It only takes a small nick in a major artery, and you can be dead within minutes.'

'But she's clean,' Sally said. 'There would be plenty of blood on the body, lots of arterial spray.'

'Perhaps she's been washed post-mortem?'

They thought about this.

'In that case, why dump her down here?' Sally murmured after a while. 'If you are going to all the trouble of cleaning her up, you are someone who is making a statement. What's the statement? What is he telling us?'

Helen Marsden was born and grew up in the U.K. She studied creative writing at City, University of London and at Sackett Street Writers in New York. She has worked as a freelance journalist and has extensive experience in HR. She's lived and travelled around the world but can usually be found in London.

hcmnyc34@gmail.com

True Things About You

Naked, she lies on her side. She's in the foetal position, then on her back. As she moves, her shiny, coral-pink toenails poke out of the pure Egyptian cotton sheets. Her smooth legs are still tanned from Barbados. She sits and stretches her arms before propping herself up on two silk-sheathed goose-down pillows. She takes a sip of water from the glass beside the super-king-sized bed, hops out, and pads to the bathroom.

Click. The curve of her spine. The small of her back. He centres the camera. A full-frontal screenshot. Zoom.

He flicks to the second camera. Her slender waist. The birthmark beside her navel. The faint web of stretch marks. Her narrow hips, the scar from two cae-sareans. She showers until steam clouds the bathroom, then opens the window to release it. She takes a fluffy, navy towel off the warm rail and uses it to buff her bronzed body. She wraps another thick towel around her head, twisting it twice. He focuses on her breasts as she brushes her teeth, watching as her left hand caresses the row of perfume bottles. She spits. Rinses. Puts the toothbrush back. He presses pause and captures a still. Click.

He lets the video footage run as she shrugs into a dark-chocolate silk gown from the back of the door, tying it neatly at the waist. She leans into the mirror to tidy her eyebrows with tweezers. Today he notices how clear her skin is, how it's hardly creased in her forty-one years. She dabs moisturiser on her carefully manicured index finger before using both hands to rub it into her cheeks, her forehead, under her slate-grey eyes.

His breath is hot and heavy in his chest as she takes a sponge to blend foun-dation in until her skin is dewy. Click. She tugs a ball of hair from her hairbrush, opens the bin with her toe, and drops it in. She runs the brush through her hon-ey-coloured hair, pulling it into a ponytail. Her ears are pierced – twice in each. She pops tiny pearls in each hole. Her diamond necklace twinkles in the light.

He watches as she sits on the toilet. As she dresses. He's been watching her for weeks. He likes to know exactly what she's doing when he's at work, during the day, the evenings, anytime he's away. Wherever he goes he can see her. He feels close to her this way.

What she doesn't know won't harm her.

CHAPTER ONE

Olivia Styles is standing in a fluffy white towelling robe making coffee. The aroma of freshly baked bread fills the kitchen. She hears the front door open and heads into the hall. Through the stained glass of the porch, she can see the shape of her husband, Russell, fully clad in Lycra. She twists the key, releases the lock, pulls the handle, and smiles at him, but only with her mouth.

He's dripping in sweat and is examining the route on Strava on his Apple watch – the latest version, of course. Behind his lithe body she can see the enthusiastic, mud-covered shape of Mabel, her tail beating rhythmically against the bristly mat. The springer spaniel greets her, has a good old shake, and leaves the walls splattered with traces of earth.

He leans in to kiss her. 'Morning.'

His stubble prickles her soft skin. She takes the peck.

'Good run? You've been gone ages. How far did you go?'

'Yes, it was a great one. All round Kingsdale Park. Mabel loved it. Lots of fox scents.' He runs his hand over his shaven head.

Olivia knows that a run in Kingsdale Park doesn't usually take Russell more than an hour but today she decides not to question him further, even though he's been gone for over two. They saunter into the kitchen. Mabel trots behind.

'Juice? Coffee?' She pulls sticks of celery off a bulb, ready for the juicer. She likes to have celery juice in the morning and a ginger-and-apple shot. She's convinced they prevent inflammation in the body.

'Both please. Bread smells great!' He stretches out his calf muscles by the patio door, his warm breath pluming in the cool air.

She plugs the juicing machine in.

'I'm working today, remember?' she says. 'I've got the charity fundraiser to plan. I need to leave at eleven-thirty latest. The architect is coming in half an hour.'

Russell is supportive of her work – it's hard not to be, since she's an unpaid Director of Fundraising for a cancer-research charity – but she suspects he'd really prefer her to be a stay-at-home mum.

He nods.

She knows he forgot, which annoys her because it was Russell who wanted these ridiculous architect-designed windows, not her.

'By the way, the sink is blocked again,' says Olivia.

'Which sink?'

'The one Mike repaired the other week. In the bedroom. Our en-suite.'

Mike is Russell's old school friend. He's useful for small jobs, but his work isn't hugely reliable and recently he's been at the house a lot – supposedly fixing things that keep breaking.

'Oh right. I'll ask him to come over again. In fact, he's popping in at the weekend,' says Russell, turning away and tapping intently at his phone.

'What for?' she says. The buzz of the juicer brings energy into the room. Foamy liquid spits out of the mouth of the machine. She pops some ginger in.

'We're planning the marathon. The Marathon des Sables.'

His shoulders hunch as he says this. He's expecting a reaction. How long has he been planning to drop this into the conversation? He'd mentioned it months ago, but they'd agreed that he wouldn't do it.

Olivia turns to face him, feeling her cheeks redden. She draws her eyebrows together.

'Are you serious, Russ? The ten-day Morocco trip? You're actually intending to do that?' She turns the juicer off and stops picking mushy fruit pulp off the counter.

Russell isn't making eye contact. He's staring into his phone. The hum of the faulty fridge-freezer drowns out the uncomfortable silence.

'So, let me get this straight.' She presses her right hand into the granite work surface and says, 'Correct me if I'm misunderstanding anything.' She starts to talk quickly, counting out the issues on her fingers.

'You are working in Chicago one week every month.' She unfolds her index finger. 'You've commissioned a swimming pool *and* architectural-designed windows, two more things we don't need.' Unfolding her middle finger, she continues: 'You're working in London Tuesday to Thursday so are only ever here at the weekend, and even on a Monday, today being a prime example, you bugger off for a run for two and a half hours and get your mother to take the kids to school on the understanding that we're spending quality time together.' Her heart rate rises as she unfolds her ring finger.

She prods her little finger. 'Then, on top of it all, you are proposing to go away with your mate for ten days right in the middle of a major house renovation?'

Her voice starts to crescendo as she runs out of fingers.

'You get twenty-five days' leave and you're going to use half of that leave, time that could be spent with your wife – and, by the way, that's me – and children, on a family holiday.' She gesticulates her anger, flinging her right arm, then the left up into the air.

'We've just been to the Caribbean, Liv. You've still got the tan,' he says, not looking up from his phone.

'Will you stop looking at that fucking thing!'

'Sorry, I am listening.'

She lets her eyes burn holes in Russell's pallid face and says, 'How about being present?'

His phone beeps. She rolls her eyes at him. She's aware that they've not paid for that holiday. She saw the credit card bill. He does this a lot. She knows that if she says anything, he will say, *I'll clear it when I get my bonus.* Besides, today she doesn't want to add in any further grievances; this is enough to deal with on a Monday morning.

'It's ten days away, Russ. On top of your work commitments. It's hard being here with the kids. I can't do everything on my own. I need support.' She rubs the dishcloth into the counter.

'I'll get my mum to help.'

'That's not the point. I want my husband here, not Kathleen. The kids want their dad here. You've just taken on that new job. You've been travelling to Chicago more and more. It's just not OK. I'm starting to wonder whether you even want to be here at all.'

'What do you mean?' He knits his eyebrows together in a frown and pulls his chin back into his neck.

'Is "Chicago" another woman?'

He turns to face her with full eye contact. 'Don't be ridiculous.'

It's true that the incessant exercising has killed his sex drive. They've not had sex for nearly three months, and that isn't unusual. New Year's Eve was the last time. *Start as you mean to go on,* they'd joked, but like most New Year's resolutions it didn't last. He doesn't initiate it. She doesn't either; she can't help wondering if he still fancies her. Or if she still fancies him.

'Ridiculous? Ridiculous is planning a ten-day trip and abandoning your family for your own selfish interests. That's what ridiculous is! The kids are too young. You also seem to have forgotten that this marathon falls on my birthday. As if that would even cross your mind.'

He clenches his jaw. 'I can fly back earlier. I've trained for this, Liv. It's always going to be your birthday whichever year I do it.'

'Nothing new, is it? You're always out. That's when you're even here.' She snorts and tosses the cloth into the sink.

'You've no idea the level of pressure I'm under at work. Absolutely no idea. You know I exercise because it helps me manage the stress. I try and keep you and the kids shielded from it, but it's not easy, Liv. OK? You're the one who wants this lifestyle as well. It's not just me,' he says wearily. He removes his glasses and places them on the counter, rubs his eyes.

'Really? I don't get time to work out. You think I want this?' she says. 'Well, you're wrong. Who's going to manage all these builders you've commissioned?'

He flinches, half turns.

'Don't walk away from me! I'm talking to you! The custom-made kitchen that "must be installed for the summer." What about that? They're starting work next week.'

He pauses and turns back but looks at her without expression. He's always been hard to argue with. His face is a blank piece of paper.

'Look, you're the one who loves cooking, baking, and entertaining, and you said you wanted a big kitchen. This is why we chose this house, remember? You *really* want to keep this pine kitchen with the brass handles?' He wrinkles his forehead at her before adding, 'I need to go and shower. The architect will be here any minute.'

Russell's phone rings.

'Sorry, got to take this. It's Faisal.'

Olivia checks her watch. Faisal is Russell's boss and he's based in Chicago. Why the hell would he be calling at this time of day? It's 4am there.

Olivia sips warm coffee as Russell showers upstairs. She stands for a moment, looks out of the patio doors onto the garden, notices how the breeze rustles the leaves. She feels the warmth of the sun on her face, shields her eyes from the light and she surveys the pony-less paddock, the moss-covered conservatory, the damp lawn. It's a beautiful place. No question. Huge. She's glad they moved here. In London they didn't even have a garden, just an uninterrupted view of the Thames. No place for bringing up kids. But she hates it here when Russell's away, which is most of the time. Rattling around in this huge house.

She heads to the porch, rubs her thumb into Mabel's fur, lets her out and watches as the spaniel rolls her filthy body on the lawn before following a delicious scent all the way down to the stream at the bottom of the garden. Mabel likes to busy herself outside for hours, rolling in mud and chasing squirrels. This is another of the benefits of living here: being able to have a dog.

Today, Olivia misses the chatter of the kids. She messages Russell's mother, Kathleen, to confirm that they got to school all right. She dismantles the juicer and empties the pulp into the bin. Once the machine is in the dishwasher with last night's dinner plates, she waits to hear the swoosh of it before heading upstairs.

In the bedroom, she notices how Russell has puffed the pillows and pulled the covers back as if they'd never slept there. She applies a full face of make-up: foundation, slate-coloured eyeliner and matching shadow, plenty of mascara, and rouge. She pulls on a pair of grey jeans, teams it with a sequinned cashmere jumper, and heads downstairs in slippered feet.

Olivia takes four free-range organic eggs from the fridge and spoons them into a pan of water, leaving them for a few minutes whilst she slices the fresh sourdough and slots a couple of pieces into the toaster. She pours her celery juice into a glass and downs it; it's the only way to do it. She sits on a high stool and savours the apple and ginger; it's sweeter and much more palatable.

The kitchen fills with the stench of burnt toast, and she wafts the smoke away with a tea towel. She opens the patio doors to freshen the air and Mabel charges in. When the eggs start to bob in the water like apples, she takes them out and puts them into egg cups. She butters the toast and cuts it in half, lays out the cutlery and plunges the coffee.

Russell is talking on the phone in his study. She stands at the door with a tray of freshly poured coffee, a juice, toast and eggs. He has his headset on and is sitting right back, as far as his specially made ergonomic chair will go. It snaps as he sits up when Olivia approaches.

He's now dressed in a pressed shirt and pin-striped tailored trousers. The shirt has a stiff collar and double cuffs, and his initials are sewn into the left-hand breast pocket in navy blue silk thread. He's always immaculate: his socks match his tie and cufflinks.

He's looking at a myriad of screens. Eight to be precise. On each screen, there are flashing graphs. He talks into his headset: 'Can I call you back?' He turns to face Olivia. 'Thank you, darling. That's lovely.' It's the closest he ever gets to an apology.

'Markets look quiet,' she says, plonking hot coffee on the walnut desk.

'Nothing's happened to move the equities market yet,' he responds in monotone and sits, stirring his coffee and staring into it as if something's floating in the cup. Russell's clients are mostly US based. UK mornings are usually pretty dead. He's not permitted to take work calls on his personal phone. It's been strictly forbidden by the financial regulator since the insider-trading scandals over a decade ago, but he has a recorded line at home and a team in London who can deal on his behalf if he wishes. However, he usually prefers to manage his own book.

Olivia glances at the paperwork on top of the filing cabinet.

'What are these?'

'What?'

'These.' She holds them up. 'School brochures.'

'I thought we could explore the idea,' he says.

Olivia flicks one open and studies it. 'I've told you. I don't want our children to go to a private school. I agreed to move up here because the local state schools are so good.'

The dog is barking from the hallway. Olivia hears footsteps on gravel.

Russell takes a call as the doorbell chimes.

'Mabel, shhhh!' Olivia rushes to the front door.

Through the stained glass she can see the shape of a man. He's shorter than Russell and his body is wider. His dark-chestnut thatch and broad shoulders are visible through the window of the outer door.

Olivia yells, 'Russ! It's the architect!'

She pulls the door open.

'Please do come in.'

'Lovely to see you again, Mrs Styles,' he says with aristocratic charm. He gives her a huge grin and offers her his large palm. He's very well built, like a rugby player – she noticed it the first time they met.

'Thank you for coming so early, Caspar.' She flashes her newly bleached teeth at him.

He's dressed in a pair of brown cords and a navy cashmere jumper with a Ralph Lauren insignia. Under his left arm he has an array of papers. He wipes his feet on the WELCOME mat in the corner of the porch and pauses to abandon his chocolate suede brogues at the door next to the row of the kids' symmetrically arranged shoes. Olivia directs him into the kitchen and ushers the dog outside.

'Coffee? Tea? Water?'

'Oh! Thank you so much. A coffee would be just wonderful. Thank you.' He smiles warmly at her. He's clean shaven and she can smell his subtle aftershave.

'Quite a project you've got here, isn't it?' he says, following her into the kitchen, his eyes flitting around the room. He pops his papers on the pine table next to the coffee cup rings and extensive crayoning, pulls off his ol-ive-green Barbour jacket and hangs it on the back of the chair.

'Yes, it really is.' Olivia gazes at the leaky patch on the ceiling where the bath overflowed, then fixes her eyes on him. As she's barely over five foot, she has to rise up on tiptoe to reach the best bone-china cups from the kitchen cabinet. They're part of the set that Russell's mum bought them as a wedding present. Kathleen's idea of course. *Important for entertaining*, she'd said. Caspar continues to beam at her and Olivia notices how his hazel eyes twinkle. He's young. Younger than Russell. Mid-thirties?

Caspar leans in for a closer look at the photograph of Olivia, Russell, eight-year-old Edie, and five-year-old Louis that hangs on the kitchen wall. It was taken last year on holiday in the Bahamas. She flicks the kettle on. Catches his eye.

'Lovely kids.'

She smiles and feels the apples of her cheeks appear. She adores her children; they're her life. She fiddles with her earring as she waits for the kettle to boil.

Russell strides in. He shakes hands with Caspar enthusiastically.

'Russell Styles. Nice to finally meet you, Mr Collinson-Smyth. My wife's been telling me all about you.' Up until now, they've only spoken on the phone.

'Please. Do call me Caspar.'

She suddenly realises that the lilies in the middle of the table make the room smell like a funeral parlour.

Russell sits opposite Olivia and Caspar. Olivia pours their coffee and adds boiling water to her cup of fresh mint leaves.

They huddle round the table and feel the warmth of the sun streaming through the double-glazed patio doors. Mabel is at the window, staring at them hopefully. A tennis ball is strategically placed between her paws. Her tail beats the newly sprouting daffodils.

Caspar opens the folded paper out onto the table to reveal the drawings for the windows. The plans curl up at the side and he runs his hands over the designs to flatten them.

'I've costed out the different options. I'll just run through each one.'

Russell stares at the drawings. Caspar takes his Mont Blanc pen and goes through them meticulously. She likes the way that he talks to them both. They've had a lot of tradespeople round who assume it's only the husband they need to win over.

'Upstairs, in the main bedroom with the en-suite, I'd recommend that you have triple glazing. It's very energy efficient. It's also great for sound-proofing. These frames are British made. See how thin they are? And they still give ultra-air tightness. A range of colours too. For you, they'd be bespoke.'

Russell nods passionately. He presses his right knuckles into the side of his face as he studies the plans. Olivia knows that he wants sound proofing. It's totally unnecessary of course. With over three acres of grounds, why would they need soundproofed windows?

'Downstairs, I'd recommend a roof lantern, with frameless windows to maximise the daylight.' Caspar flicks through a brochure and points to a picture. 'See this one, this is what I was thinking for here. This is solar glass. It has a special film which filters glare.'

'Wow,' says Russell. 'So much light! Look at that, Liv. Imagine what that will be like on a sunny day.' Shoving his ankle up onto his knee, he sits back.

Olivia tries to hide her disbelief. She was the one who refused to offer on a Grade II listed house because the windows weren't big enough and planning didn't allow for any alterations, so she knows that Russell is pulling her strings. He often does this. The windows do look amazing. No question about it. But really? None of this is needed.

'My wife is concerned about security, as am I. We need a full system upgrade. Could you run us through the options on that front? Locks and bolts and so on. I'm also keen on sensors and lighting in the garden,' says Russell.

It's true that Olivia still worries about this. They were burgled when they lived in London. They're much more isolated here. She refused to move in until the alarm was installed, and that's also how she managed to persuade Russell to get a dog.

'Security is not my field, but I can arrange that too. So, the costs.' Caspar has an A3 page. He's holding it up to his olive skin. 'The triple glazing is standard. The tilt and turn windows are extra. For the upstairs it will be sixty-seven thousand, seven hundred and eighty-nine pounds plus VAT. If you decide not to have the additional sound proofing, solar and privacy glass, it will be fifteen percent less. Downstairs, the costs are forty-three thousand, two hundred and sixty-three pounds plus VAT. If you do both, I can give you a further eight-percent discount.'

All the blood drains from Olivia's face. She feels sick. More than a little sick. This is a lot of money. She doesn't think they can afford it. But truth be told she simply doesn't know enough about their finances. Why should she? Russell is the one with the economics degree, not her. She's always kept out of the finances, what he gets paid. Besides, they always seem to have enough.

'What do you think?' asks Caspar. He looks right at them and flashes his straight, even teeth.

'I'm keen,' says Russell.

Now there's a surprise.

'I think we need to discuss this, look at the budgets, and let Mr Collinson-Smyth, I mean, Caspar, know,' says Olivia, sipping on her mint tea. She's not going to let him sign up to it without discussing it with her first.

Russell stands. It's clear he's already decided. He smiles at Caspar, shakes his hand, and says, 'Thank you so much for all your work on this. You've done a fantastic job. I need to be getting back to my desk, I'm afraid. The markets are calling. Thank you, we will be in touch.' Russell heads off towards his office.

'Please do finish your coffee,' says Olivia, noticing that Caspar's not touched it. 'Is it warm enough? Would you like another one?'

'Oh no, thank you. I'd better get going. Very nice to see you again.'

Once she's seen Caspar out, Olivia peers round the door of Russell's office. She folds her arms at him. She can see the angst on his face.

'What about we get the windows done before I go and then you can relax a bit more about the security?' He swivels the chair around and sits legs akimbo.

'It's the worst possible time. And you were away when we had the whole house rewired last year, remember? Bedrooms, bathrooms, everything!'

'My family's safety is very important.'

'Where the hell are we going to get all that money from?'

'I'll sort it.'

She feels her eyes widen as her carefully threaded eyebrows shoot up.

'We still haven't paid for Barbados, Russ.'

He colours. 'I'll sort them both. It's fine, I have the money coming.'

'It's not just about security.' She feels her heart rate accelerating again. She fiddles with her necklace to try and steady it. 'I don't like to be on my own. What happens if we get burgled again?'

'I'll get my mother to stay over when I'm in Morocco.' He crosses his legs.

She's silent. Her eyes continue to burn holes in his head.

'I'll raise money for Survivors.'

Her charity. Clever. He knows it's her weak spot, she'll do anything for the cause close to her heart. She lost her mother to cancer when she was just eight years old, and it's a cause she feels passionate about, one she throws as much of herself into as she can. After they married, she gave up her job as a primary school teacher to devote her time to fundraising.

'How about that? I should easily get a few thousand. Possibly tens. It will be amazing.'

For a moment she's taken back to when they were dating, when he made life seem so easy and he reassured her about everything.

'Oh! So, you're doing me a favour now? You're making it seem like it's not a big deal when you know full well it is.'

He holds up a finger, presses a button on the trading platform, and talks into his headset.

She walks out of the room shaking her head. She knows he won't listen. She knows he'll just go ahead and do it anyway. What she says won't make any difference. He's been behaving even more remotely than ever. Where was he for over two hours this morning? She could look at his Strava. Just to reassure herself. He's downloaded his Strava data onto the laptop and there's no passcode on that. But she doesn't want to have a relationship where she has to check up on her husband. No, that really doesn't feel right at all.

But where is he getting all this money from?

Olivia heads back into the kitchen, stands hand on hip, swirls the last drop of minty water around her cup, and downs it. She puts the crockery into the sink, runs water into it and swooshes it around until the bubbles come. She rubs away at the bone-china cups with their gold rims, dipping them in and out of the soapy liquid before carefully lining them up on the draining board. She usually leaves the washing-up to Russell – she could never get the counters clean enough and, even if she did, his obsession with hygiene would have him scrubbing at them again anyway. The arrangement is she cooks, he cleans. When he's here.

Olivia dries her hands on the stripey tea towel that's draped on the oven, shoves school shirts into the washer, slings on her puffy jacket from the hook in the hall and pushes her feet into her pale-pink suede heels. She reaches into her bag for her lipstick and rolls it over her lips until they turn cherry, drops her phone into her grey calf-skin handbag, and yells, 'Russ, can you hang the shirts up when the wash finishes? I've got to go to my meeting now.' Before he has a chance to reply, she's already heading out the door.

Through the open window, she can hear Russell on the phone. As a private banking customer, he has his own relationship manager.

'Yes, I know. I know. I'm fully aware of my credit card balances. And the loan. Yes, *loans*. You must appreciate I am expecting a very large bonus this year, larger than I've seen before. My revenue has been phenomenal, and we are going to invest it in the house. It will all add to the value, so there's nothing for you to worry about.'

In the downstairs loo, Olivia has her back to the door. He watches as she gets up, naked from the waist down. She pulls a strip of loo roll and puts her hand in between her legs. As she turns and drops it into the bowl, he gets a full view of her neatly trimmed pubic hair. Everything manicured and perfect.

Kit Morrell has seen a ghost, witnessed a dying breath and held a human heart. Inspired by these privileged experiences and her medical and pharmaceutical background, she writes crime fiction and poetry. Her work has been shared locally and globally by healthcare organisations and on radio. *Death Scent* is her first novel.

kit.morrell@outlook.com

Death Scent
The opening chapter of a crime thriller

CHAPTER ONE
Evan – November, 2012

I have peanuts in my head.

Not ready salted or dry roasted but multifocal white matter lesions. These exactly peanut-shaped areas that have set up shop in my brain are the reason that I can smell things that no-one else can. As my head pulses, it creates a rhythmic tune in my head: a sick backing track that repeats as I stare at the carved letters on the wooden memorial plaque. A year. A year since their bodies were lowered into the cold earth. I can smell it, the repulsive scent of death. It clings to the air, heavy, like a thick cloak.

The musky odour of bones and tissues, a pulpy mess of cells that have been slowly putrefied, is unique and unmistakable. It demands my instant and undivided attention. Like a petulant child, it's determined to get noticed. I'm doing my utmost to ignore it, to focus instead on the reason I am here.

I can hardly fathom what's left of them now is part of the soil and earth, the fabric of this woodland burial park that is their resting place. She would have wanted them to be a part of nature, the circle of life. Far better than a morbid cemetery. The vibrant colours of the flowers I have left will melt into the landscape soon enough. I think of their physical remains as the fleshy overcoats they wore in life. Nothing more. Their essence, their spirit, is always with me. They're not gone.

Bitter wind whips my face with shards of freezing rain as I carefully place a large white pebble at the feet of two wooden hand-sculpted robins. It will remain next to all the other pebbles that I have left before. Each a reminder of the gaping hole the loss has left in my life. Each stone a symbol of loneliness and a million unanswered questions. Little white soldiers, silently keeping watch.

The police officer's words are etched into me, gouged into my soul. So blunt, so brutal. No emotion, just the facts. The moment they left his mouth, my world stopped turning on its axis. Everything hung suspended in a surreal vacuum.

Dead.

It's a simple enough word, yet I had no knowledge then of the devastation it would bring. It was hard to take it in. I'm doing my best to face the life-altering truth. They're not coming back. Nothing will ever be the same again.

When it first happened, I couldn't accept that they were gone. My anger was savage, primal and all-consuming: it gnawed at my innards like a rat. I was angry that she was even there that day. Angry that she didn't listen to me. Angry that she'd left me. Endless questions lapped, ebbing and flowing, always there. They're still there. Why us? Why then? Why... why?

I don't believe she fell, that it was an accident. I didn't believe it a year ago, I don't believe it now. I have to know what happened. The few fragments that I've managed to piece together just don't add up. I can't move on until I'm satisfied, until I know it all.

I force myself to keep going, to face each day without them, knowing what our lives should have been. I see other couples with new-born babies and it rips at my guts. I try not to despise them for their happiness, the joy that we should have had. It's not their fault. I either accept it or else lose myself in the darkness.

My phone rings in my pocket, ripping me away from my thoughts. Annoyed at myself for not switching it off, I tug it out.

'Evan, where are you? I'm sure we arranged to meet at eight? Buddy must've peed his furry pants by now,' a familiar voice says.

'Christ. Sorry Kim... be there in ten,' I reply. I slowly crouch down and brush away untidy twigs and soggy leaves with my hand. I bring two fingers to my lips, kiss them and place them on the carved letters. I love you. I miss you.

I walk away resisting the urge to look back. I know if I do, it only makes leaving them harder. Instead, I put my head down, jam my hands in my pockets and concentrate on putting one foot in front of the other.

My car's tucked in the corner of the small car park: it's the only one here at this time in the morning. Opening the door, I'm hit by Buddy's lamb and beefy chunks breath. More Bernese sofa dog than mountain dog, his huge hundred-pound frame fills every square centimetre of my ancient Fiat. Wearing the car like a metal gillet, he watches me as I swing the door back and forth on its hinges to dissipate the smell. Blackbirds are sitting on the telephone wire that sags between its tall wooden poles.

Dark silhouettes in the morning mist: standing to attention, lined up in an orderly row, as if waiting for something.

I turn the key in the ignition and the radio comes to life. Our song. I couldn't have timed it better if I'd choreographed it. What are the odds? I remember the two of us in my car waiting to glimpse the sunrise, singing along together. So young, so ignorant of what was to come.

I drive for only a few miles before turning left down a narrow lane. Finally, I squeeze my car between two narrow posts which form the entrance to Whellendale Woods. The rain is easing off. I take in a long deep breath: in through my nose, out through my mouth and try and relax my shoulders. Grabbing my muddy wellies from the boot, I clip Buddy's lead to his collar and rush to where Kim is waiting. We're all frosted hurried breaths and apologies. Buddy's tongue hanging out like a pink flip flop, he circles Kim's legs. He loves Kim, unashamedly flirts with her. I think it's the doggy biscuits she has hidden in her pocket for later that cements the attraction. Kim's Alsatian, Belle, trails behind Buddy, sniffing, wagging her tail and bumping her nose against him.

'Sorry. You look frozen solid,' I say as I rub my hands together before pulling on my gloves. 'Let's get a wiggle on.'

'I can't believe it's a year,' she says, placing her mittened hand on my arm. Her dark hair has gone curly in the damp morning air and her cheeks are flushed. She's one of the few people I can stand to be with today.

We walk in comfortable silence. Fluttering leaves on tall oaks rustle in the cold wind. A woodpecker is drumming the familiar sound of the countryside. Earthy moss, peaty soil and Kim's perfume create an interesting mix and the scent does little to improve my banging head. Peck. Peck. Peck.

'Did you know that woodpeckers have shock-absorbent tissue between the base of the bill and the skull to cushion the impact of drumming? Stops them getting a headache,' I say.

'Ev, you're such an anorak!' Kim chuckles.

'You can talk,' I say. 'Dazzling with your stories of ingrown toenails and anal fissures.'

We walk quite a way, what must be a few miles, when I sense an odour that worries the inside of my nostrils. What's that stench? Buddy wanders off the path, his spongy nose sniffing the air. His shape, a steaming mass of black, white and tan fluff, grows smaller and smaller as he disappears from view.

'Buddy... get back here or you're in big trouble!' I shout. Kim always finds it amusing that I talk to him like a human. 'Little sod. He's probably seen a squirrel. Can you smell that?'

'No, I can't smell anything. Belle... come!' Kim yells.

We head off the worn path and scramble over a barbed wire fence as the dogs run ahead of us. A pungent and familiar smell is getting stronger the further we walk. We're in the grounds of the old Leavesdale Psychiatric Hospital that backs onto the woods. We used to play here when we were kids. Hated the place, spooky as hell. I'm sure I read something about it being developed into a new community-friendly space. Ugly diggers are scattered around the place, idle and caked in mud. There are buildings from every era, none of which will be winning an outstanding architecture award. The exception is the mansion house. It stands erect like a Victorian gentlewoman, all straight lace and everything in its correct proportions.

We keep walking until we reach a low squat building with a no-nonsense sign that reads MORTUARY. The smell I sensed back on the path has grown eye-wateringly pungent: sickly-sweet and putrid, it's making me want to retch. Buddy, low to the ground, ears pinned back, is growling as he scratches at the half-open door. The swollen wood is keeping it in place. Kim tries to calm him, puts both dogs on their leads and pulls them away as they push to get inside.

'God, that smell is awful. Be careful Evan,' Kim warns as she brings her hand up to pinch her nose.

'I'll just take a peek... see where the stench is coming from,' I say as I peer into the darkness. 'It's probably a dead fox or something.'

Putting my weight behind the partially open door with my boot, I shove it far enough that I can glance further inside. I breathe in the foul air. There is nothing but black and the all-pervasive fetid stench. My brain scrambles to decipher the rancid mix. Candle wax, a burning match, salt, a hint of a drug I recognise, blood, urine, all floating in the air like free spirits.

The world seems to pitch sideways as my vision blurs and I almost lose my footing. Pictures form in my mind: quick snapshots and then they're gone. A child in the back of a car looking through the window. Small hands pressed to the glass. The mansion house slowly fading from view. The images form wispy clouds in my subconscious mind. Like broken fragments of a dream but in the here and now.

'Christ, it's dark,' I begin before my eyes adjust. I recoil. 'Kim, we need to call the police. It's a body.'

'What? Oh my God.' I hear her gasp.

I can just make out the outline of a man's body. His arms are spread out to each side, his legs together. I fumble my phone from my pocket and use the torch. I slowly scan the tiny light across the room trying to take in as much detail as possible. The man's mouth gapes open, a white crystalline substance just visible inside. His eyes look odd, inhuman; a fixed and emotionless stare. There are livid marks round his neck, something tied tight digging into his boggy flesh. His fingers are sticking out at odd angles like a country road sign showing the way.

'Tell them it looks like he's been murdered,' I shout. I see two pools of wax with a black stump of wick in the middle on the concrete floor. I catch my breath, try to slow my breathing. Discarded next to the body is a black pen: I can just make out a familiar white star logo. I remember buying the same slimline design with gold trim. I suck in short sharp breaths. It can't be. No way. I'm imagining things.

The man's face is deeply wrinkled: his urine-soaked trousers are stretched over a doughy belly, his grey hair sparse and combed over, liver spots on his hands. I don't venture further into the room, but back away carefully. I try not to disturb the door on my exit.

'Whatever happened here, it certainly wasn't an accident,' I say as I do my best to stop my hands shaking.

'Come and sit over here... take a few deep breaths,' Kim says as she ushers me to some nearby steps. 'I'll check if there's any vital signs, see if there's anything I can do.' She has moved into doctor mode, hurries to the door. I catch her arm, pull her back.

'Trust me. He's dead. We need to preserve the scene. If you go in, it could compromise any forensics.' I've spent enough late nights talking over Will's cases to know we must stay back.

'I won't disturb anything. I have to see with my own eyes,' Kim insists as she peers in through the door. For a few moments she stands completely motionless, fixed to the spot, trance-like. She steps away pulling her arms tight against her body to avoid snagging her coat. I wanted to spare her the brutality.

We perch ourselves under a corrugated metal roof that hangs over the steps of a small brick building, dogs on their leads at our side. Big rain drops begin to bounce loudly overhead, deafening us as we wait.

'I'll phone work, tell them I'll be late. God, what a bloody nightmare,' I say.

'I'll do the same. There's no telling how long this will take. Poor man. What a way to go.' Kim takes off her scarf and wraps it round my neck.

We wait for the police to arrive, watching the rain fall, the roof above us creaking as the wind catches its edge. We try to speak to one another, but our words are whipped from our mouths as they blow away in the wind. After about fifteen minutes, I see a white car with distinct blue and yellow markings approach along the un-made road that crosses in front of the mortuary. It pulls up sharp and a solidly built young officer in uniform hurries over to us trying to side-step the puddles. The other passenger, a short officer with spiked ginger hair, saunters towards the mortuary.

'Morning. You two the ones who called 999?' he says as rain drips on his police vest. 'The dispatcher said something about a body?'

'Yes, it was us who made the call. We were out walking our dogs... followed them here... they'd picked up a scent. We haven't touched anything... called you the moment we realised there was a body,' I blurt out. 'It's over there, just inside the building.' I point my extended index finger in the direction of his colleague.

'OK, right... well... if you wouldn't mind waiting here, we'll take a look,' he says. Buddy lets out a low growl and shows his teeth. He senses something is very wrong. We watch the officer tip-toe through the mud before he and his colleague peer round the edge of the door. Their reaction is swift. The ginger officer talks into his police radio, his partner hurries to the car, opens the boot and pulls out a reel of police tape.

Struggling with the wind and rain whipping the tape into their faces, the two officers hurriedly secure the mortuary's perimeter. Kim and I are motioned to come over.

'Can you take a seat in the back of the car please? We'll need to take some details,' the ginger officer says as rain drips off the end of a nose that looks as though it's taken a few punches in its time.

Kim and I shuffle across the plastic back seat of the police car and the dogs squeeze next to us. We're all a steamy mess. The car reeks of greasy burgers, sweet drinks and old sweat. There's a lingering acidic heart note of vomit mixed with alcohol and a chlorine-like base note of bleach that must have been used in an attempt to cover it up. Kim's nose wrinkles at the edges. I'm comforted that for once it isn't only me that can detect the uninviting aroma. I dread to think of the characters who have been in here.

The chunkier of the two officers slides into the driver's seat.

'Can you state your name, occupation, contact details and what transpired this morning?' he says from the front of the vehicle. His breath tells me he's had coffee and a bacon butty for breakfast. There's something else? Infection. I can only assume it's from a dental abscess, or perhaps tonsilitis, who knows? Either way, it's not nice and his cheap aftershave does little to disguise it. I rub my finger on the glass, making it squeak, and look out of the steamy window to distract myself as Kim patiently answers his questions.

Twenty minutes pass and I hear police sirens in the distance and unmarked vehicles with blue lights flashing start to arrive. Plain clothes officers are talking to the soaked-through ginger constable whose once meticulously spiked hair is now plastered flat to his head. Out of the back of a police van, a man in a white paper suit, mask, blue gloves and shoe covers, appears with a camera dangling from one shoulder. There are vehicles and people everywhere.

A silver Mercedes AMG GT pebble-dashes the morgue building as it comes to an abrupt stop. A perky blonde woman jumps out of the driver's side. I can smell the rose, geranium and musk of her perfume as it wafts through the vents in the dashboard. It smells expensive. French, I suspect. What looks like a well-practiced routine unfolds as she quickly wrestles into her crime scene regalia. She hurries towards the flapping tape, a silver medical bag in one hand. On her heels are more white-suited personnel carrying lamps, foot plates and bags of equipment: an advancing platoon of white smurfs.

A man in a long navy raincoat who introduces himself as Detective Sergeant Fox, struggles into the passenger side of the car. I recognise him. He's one of Will's team. I met him once at the pub when Will and I were out having a pint. He remembers me and we exchange a brief greeting. His manner is courteous and professional: he impresses upon us the need to get our more detailed statements as soon as possible, whilst it's still fresh in our minds. We agree to attend the police station in an hour so we can drop the dogs off on our way and dry ourselves off. Better to get it over with.

We trudge back to the path with Buddy and Belle on their leads. We're bouncing ideas around about what has happened, a verbal ping pong, asking questions, back and forth. Who was the poor sod lying on the floor of the mortuary? Was he just in the wrong place at the wrong time?

'Why don't you follow me back to my place? We can grab a coffee? Leave Belle at the cottage until later... head to the station together if you like?'

'Sounds fine. Is it wrong to feel like I need something stronger than a coffee? Do you have any brandy? I feel like an old lady who needs a dose of smelling salts,' Kim replies.

My head is pounding so badly, it's making me feel nauseous. The sooner I can get home and take some pills the better. Arriving back at my car, Buddy senses my darkening mood and squeezing into the back seat, he slumps himself down with a grunt. Like me, I think he wants to get back to the safety of our little cottage, curl up in his bed. Try and lock the evil out.

Smoky bacon crisps, cheese and onion sandwiches, stale sweat and industrial floor cleaner create an olfactory fog. The pungent institutional mix transports me back to my school days. Lines of jostling boys' bodies, pushing and shoving in the lunch queue. As Kim and I walk down the otherwise vacant main corridor of the police station, the double doors ahead of us swing open revealing Will. All white teeth, fashionably neat five-o-clock shadow and expensive suit, he stops and looks at us, incredulous.

'Mate... what the fuck? Hiya, Kim... I just heard. You OK, you look like crap?' he says.

'Thanks a bunch. Don't look so hot yourself... you look knackered.'

'Christ, Ev... can't leave you alone for five minutes without some drama happening,' he replies. He seems different, distracted, says he'll try and join us when we give our statements if he can. His usual vitality, his get up and go, seems to have got up and gone.

Kim and I eventually find where we're supposed to be and are escorted to separate interview rooms. I am asked to recount every minute detail of what happened this morning. How often do I walk near the hospital? Who else did I see? Exactly when did I come upon the body? Did I touch anything? How was the body positioned? Every vital snippet of information teased out, filling in the blanks; like doing a puzzle without a picture on the box to guide you.

I've tried to explain the weird sensations and feelings I experienced in the mortuary. Will, who has eventually joined us, struggles to process my unusual interpretations. So do I. He's such a black and white thinker at the best of times. My new affliction, for want of a better word, has been pressing all of his buttons. My enhanced senses are difficult to explain in words, even to myself, let alone someone else. It's only been this bad for the past couple of months, so I'm struggling to make sense of it. Will is used to dealing in cold hard facts. I've tried to explain what I could smell, the strange snapshots I saw in my mind. The moment Will's colleague leaves us to answer his phone, he makes the most of the opportunity to inform me I've lost my grasp on reality: refers to my explanations as woo-woo bullshit. Twat.

I've consumed too many cups of unpleasant brown liquid masquerading as coffee and my nerves are jangling and buzzing. I step out of the interview room and remember I'm supposed to be operating this afternoon. A

Maine Coon's hip replacement and a spinal fusion on a Poodle have had to be delayed and they can't wait forever. I just hope they've managed to re-schedule the operating theatre or there's going to be some stroppy phone calls later. I locate my mobile and jab my finger on the tiny blue plane as Kim appears from the adjacent room.

'I'll quickly call the office. We can get back to the cottage so you can pick up Belle,' I say. She looks as bored and frustrated as I feel.

'Thanks. I have a full list of patients this afternoon so I need to get back to the practice.' Everyday life and commitments don't just stop because a life has been lost. Kim looks pale and strung out. Should she be heading home rather than to work? I understand though, people rely on us.

'You OK? It's been a bit full on all of this. Couldn't one of your colleagues cover your list? It's not like this sort of thing happens every day.' I know I'm wasting my breath.

'No, I'm fine. To be honest the thought of going home and remembering this morning freaks me out. I'm better to stay busy, take my mind off things.' Told you so.

'If you're sure? At least let's grab a decent cup of coffee first?' I shrug on my damp jacket.

'Deal.' For the first time since finding the body, a glimpse of a smile forms. We walk together towards the exit at the end of the corridor. Biting cold air hits us in the face as we swing through the double doors. The drizzly weather suits my mood as we retrieve my Fiat from the crammed-full car park. I slump into the driver's seat and turn the key.

'Can't get the picture of the body out of my mind,' I say to Kim who has lowered the passenger window. Does the car still stink of Buddy? I hope not.

'Same... it's different when you see a dead body at work,' Kim replies as she picks at a hangnail on her thumb.

We drive for fifteen minutes or so before the familiar crunch of tires on gravel heralds our arrival and I am momentarily calmed by the sight of the quintessential thatched roof and white gate. I am relieved to see the tiny ancient building that I call home. The gate is swinging on its hinges. Did I shut it? I'm sure I did, I remember locking it behind me. I always do. Perhaps the wind caught the latch or someone delivering junk mail has left it open? I can hear Buddy barking as I open the car door: a loud guttural sound punctuated with whimpering and growling. What's the matter, boy? I don't like what my sense of smell is telling me either.

My fingers fumble with the stiff lock of the front door. For fuck's sake. I step onto the ancient flagstones and the ferrous smell of blood catches in my throat. Buddy hurls himself at me almost knocking me off my feet. What the hell? The small console table where I discard my post slams hard against the wall. I can see large bloody paw prints that create a repeating pattern on the stone. Frantically running my hands over Buddy, I can feel only warm fur, no clues as to where the blood is coming from. For a fraction of a second, I get a faint waft of Ashna's perfume and then in an instant it's gone and a cold breeze is left in its wake.

'Where's Belle?' Kim asks as she rushes past me into the hall.

'Be careful. Wait for me,' I say.

'Evan, come quickly. It's Belle,' she shouts from the kitchen.

Belle is lying on the floor in a puddle of sticky blood, her fur wet and spiky. A motionless mass of scarlet stained fluff. Her pale grey tongue is flopped out to the side of her mouth. Her ribcage is expanding and straining as she struggles to take short sharp breaths. I see a tiny flick of her furry eyebrows as she attempts but fails to open her eyes. Her lower abdomen is slashed open. Coiled shiny loops of intestine are gaping from the wound which hangs open like a huge angry mouth. A damp meaty odour redolent of an abattoir pervades the air mixed with the same scent I detected at the mortuary.

In my peripheral vision, I notice the back door lock is framed by splintered wood and white flakes of paint are scattered on the ground like snow. Large footprints this time. Human. They leave a trail as they exit the back door.

'Oh my God, Belle, Belle.' Kim is kneeling, her body heaving as she sobs. We see it at the same time: the black handle of a knife pointing out from underneath the kitchen island. The half-hidden metal shaft glistens and red smears stick to the blade. I don't recognise it as belonging to the set sitting on the kitchen counter and I note that none are missing. Could whoever has done this have brought the knife with them? Did one of the dogs go for them?

Grabbing the tea-towel that sits draped over the Aga rail, I apply firm pressure as I try to stem the bleeding. Warm blood oozes between my fingers. I feel static in the air.

'Kim!' My sharp tone snaps her back into the moment. 'Take over compressing the wound. I need to call the hospital.' Belle could bleed out right here on my kitchen floor.

My phone slithers and slides in my bloody hands as I frantically scroll to my office number. Buddy's warm body is pressed into my legs, seeking comfort and reassurance. He makes slurping sounds as his big tongue licks the air nervously. The white parts of his coat and muzzle are crimson. He must've licked Belle, comforting her as she lay fighting for her life.

'Simon. Evan here. I have a code red trauma, an Alsatian with an eviscerating abdominal wound. I need a theatre and a full team. We won't have time for imaging. We'll be there in the next ten minutes.'

'We'll be waiting,' he says.

I take the stairs two at a time, grab towels from the airing cupboard. Piles of sheets and pillow cases fall as I snatch them out and then scramble down and into the kitchen. Kim, tears streaming down her cheeks, blood soaked into her jeans, grabs them from me and applies pressure. She shuffles and slips to one side so that she can jam the brushed cotton against the gaping slit. I scoop up Belle's limp frame. She's heavy. I can barely hold her full weight. Kim slides her free hand under Belle's dangling back legs and we struggle her to the car. Kim squeezes into the back seat and we lay Belle across her lap.

'Good boy, Bud. Come on.' The words whispered and audible only to us as I slam the door with my foot. Buddy inches his huge frame into the front seat as he rides shotgun. Something is different. He normally sits in the back. I slam my car into gear. Questions about the murder and what has happened to Belle bounce round my synapses like a pinball as I drive.

The hospital comes into view and I screech my car up to the back doors. I'm beyond grateful and relieved that my trusted colleagues are prepped and waiting. A bundle of bodies and hands, a clinical scrum, we carefully lift Belle from the back seat of the car. Kim is shooshing and speaking in soft tones to her beloved pet. One hand stroking her head tenderly, the other pinning the towels against Belle's abdomen.

'It's OK, sweetie. We're here now. You're going to be OK. Be brave little one.'

ACKNOWLEDGEMENTS

This anthology contains work from the 2022 cohort of the UEA MA in Creative Writing Crime Fiction that persevered in spite of a global pandemic. The fortitude and determination that shaped these novels also shapes the thanks we would like to give to those who helped us navigate a world of video calls, digital communications and limited social interaction.

To start with, we are hugely grateful to Lee Child for writing the foreword and to Tom Benn for the introduction. What gifts from such inspirational and talented crime writers!

We would like to thank our course tutors – Henry Sutton, Nathan Ashman, Tom Benn, Julia Crouch and Jake Huntley – for their support, insights and brave navigation of all things digital to bring us an impressive two-year experience. We are extra grateful to Henry and Nathan for convening the course.

The course convenors brought us an incredible list of talent for our Masterclasses. Our thanks go to Janice Hallett, Mari Hannah, Jacob Ross, Cath Staincliffe, Harriet Tyce, and Cathi Unsworth for sharing their experience and insights, and for inspiring us to be even more passionate about writing. Thanks also to Graham Bartlett for sharing his extensive police expertise and to Justine Mann from the British Archive for Contemporary Writing for a fascinating look into the Lee Child archive.

Since so much of our course was online, we are also very thankful for Andy Mee's IT support and Grant Young's library support.

We are grateful for the visiting agents and publishers who gave so generously of their time: Diana Beaumont, Katie Brown, Kate Burke, Isobel Dixon, David Headley, Allegra Le Fanu, Anna Power, Ruth Tross and Ed Wood.

Thanks also to Philip Langeskov; Emily Benton Book Design; and the UEA School of Literature, Drama and Creative Writing in partnership with Egg Box Publishing, because without them this anthology would not exist. And to the editorial committee – Asun Álvarez, Nina Bhadreshwar, Kat Latham, Tamsin Mackay and Helen Marsden – as well as a special mention to Julia Bordin, for their hard work and dedication. Thanks also go to the scholarships and prizes that support some of our writers, including the PG UEA Brazil Award, PG UEA Sub-Saharan Africa Award, and the Little, Brown UEA Crime Fiction Award.

Thank you to the fantastic events team and all the amazing authors they bring to the Noirwich Crime Writing Festival. During our two years on the course, Attica Locke and Megan Abbott inspired us with their Noirwich lectures, and many others led brilliant sessions that we learned so much from.

We are incredibly grateful to the family and friends who supported us while we were writing a novel and completing a master's degree during a pandemic. These years have not been easy, and we couldn't have done it without your love and encouragement.

Finally, thanks go to all our fellow students – for the friendship, the patience, the kindness, the margin notes and the brainstorming sessions. Here's to your future writing successes!

UEA MA Creative Writing Anthologies: Crime Fiction

First published by Egg Box Publishing, 2022
Part of the UEA Publishing Project Ltd.

International © retained by individual authors

A CIP record for this book is available from the British Library
Printed and bound in the UK by Imprint Digital

Designed by Emily Benton Book Design
emilybentonbookdesign.co.uk

Distributed by NBN International
10 Thornbury Road
Plymouth
PL6 7PP
+44 (0)1752 202 301
e.cservs@nbninternational.com

ISBN 978-1-913861-81-0